〈27〉

THE GIRLS
OF CANBY HALL

THE ROOMMATE
AND
THE COWBOY

EMILY CHASE

SCHOLASTIC INC.
New York Toronto London Auckland Sydney

ISBN 0-590-41930-2

12 11 10 9 8 7 6 5 4 3 2 1   8 9/8 0 1 2 3/9

Printed in the U.S.A.   01

First Scholastic printing, April 1988

27

THE GIRLS OF CANBY HALL

THE ROOMMATE AND THE COWBOY

THE GIRLS
OF CANBY HALL

Chapter One

The hot Texas wind tossed Toby's red curls as she trotted her horse Max to a stop. She lifted one booted foot from the stirrup and drew it across her saddle, resting it on her opposite knee. Absentmindedly, she reached down and patted Max on the neck while her bright green eyes studied the miles of empty Texas flatlands that surrounded her.

"What's wrong with me, fella?" she asked. Max, knowing the voice of his beloved Toby, perked up his ears. "The whole time I was at Canby Hall, I couldn't wait to get back to this place. All I wanted to do was climb on your back and ride for miles. And here we are, just the two of us. Nothing looks like it's changed, but it all feels different somehow."

She stared at the dry, broken landscape. Texas was hot in August. She could almost see heat rising up around her. There were

1

few shade trees on the open range. Mostly scruffy little mesquite bushes dotted the prairie in a never-ending jumble all the way to El Paso.

Toby hoisted her leg over the saddle horn and wedged her foot back into the stirrup. She nudged her heels gently into Max's side and made a clicking sound with her tongue before giving Max his head. He took off and Toby felt herself almost flying over the plains. Her body cut through the hot, dry air which was evaporating the perspiration that had gathered in little beads on her tanned face.

Riding up to the house, Toby felt her heart swell with love for the old, familiar ranch house. Toby had seen pictures of the house when it had been all white, but she only remembered it as the weathered brown it was now. The trim was still white and had to be painted nearly every summer to stay that way.

The two-story house was surrounded with a large, comfortable wrap-around porch that held an old porch swing as well as worn wicker furniture where Toby had spent countless summer evenings listening to the night sounds of the prairie. She loved this place. The idea that it was home overrode the feelings of emptiness she'd had earlier.

Toby took care of Max and put him in the corral and went into the house. The silence was interrupted only by the soft whirring of the ceiling fans as they sliced into the hot air and spun it into a cool breeze.

Toby flopped into a chair, her long legs spread out in front of her, her arms draped out at either side of her, her eyes closed. She let the air blow across her. The creak of the front door startled her, and she jumped up so fast she almost slid onto the floor.

"Caught you napping, huh?" her father asked with a smile.

"No, just cooling off."

"Been out on Max, I see."

"Yeah."

"He missed you this year. I tried to get out there and ride him, but it just wasn't the same." Toby's father was a big man. His muscular frame had been hardened by working on the ranch, but he always appeared younger than his forty-one years. Since Toby came home, though, she'd noticed a tinge of silver in his light brown hair when the sun caught it just right.

Her dad nodded his head toward the kitchen. "How about some lunch?"

Toby followed her father into the kitchen. He got out the cold chicken left over from the night before. Toby got out the rest of the potato salad and baked beans. She put the beans in the oven and set the table while they were warming up.

"I'll call Abe," Toby said. She opened the back door, picked up the thin metal stick and expertly spun it around in the triangle hanging from the back porch. She had always loved that old triangle. When she was too small to reach it, she had pulled a chair over and climbed precariously to whatever height it had taken to ring out the sound that announced dinner to the men in the bunkhouse. Of course, this time of year there was no one but Abe, her father's right-hand man who had been with them forever.

Abe came out of the bunkhouse pushing his shirt into the top of his jeans. Toby jumped from the porch and went out to meet him. Abe was probably just a little older than her father, she guessed, and she loved him almost as much as she loved her dad. He dropped his big arm behind her and encircled her slim waist. "I think, little girl, them Yankees are starving you plum to death back east."

"Abe, I'm the same size I've always been. I just got taller, so I look thinner." They climbed the steps of the back porch and went through the screen door into the kitchen.

Toby dug in with an appetite almost as hearty as Abe's and her father's. True, she could eat the Canby Hall food better than anybody else, but there was nothing quite like good home cooking.

Thinking about Canby Hall brought back memories of Andy and Jane. What were they doing today? Was it hot where they were?

She could almost picture Jane sitting in the formal dining room, picking daintily at a light garden salad. Or Andy sitting at the table in the kitchen at the family's restaurant, trying some new dessert her mother had just taken out of the oven. She looked at the food still lying on her plate and wasn't hungry anymore. She pushed her chair back and got to her feet.

"You finished?" her father asked. "There's apple pie."

"Maybe later." Toby took her plate from the table and set it in the sink. When Abe and her father finished, and Toby had cleaned up the kitchen, she walked through the silent house. There was nothing to do.

Toby went out front and sat on the porch swing, listening to the buzzing cicadas in the distance. She hadn't been home that long and she was bored already. How was she going to stand the weeks of loneliness before school began?

Without really knowing how or when it happened, Toby had gotten used to people. Her father had sent her off to school to learn how to get along with people, and she guessed it had worked even better than he'd hoped.

Jane Barrett sat on the terrace of her family's town house in Boston and picked at the mixed fruit salad she was eating. It was all fresh fruit and probably very tasty, but right now she would have traded it for a soggy tuna salad and a pickle slice from the Canby Hall cafeteria.

She stood up and looked out at the lawn behind their town house. A gardener was busy trimming the shrubs. She watched him intently. As if he felt her eyes on him, he looked up and caught her staring at him.

Jane gave him a feeble wave. He stared bewilderedly at her for a moment, trying to recognize the slim blonde girl on the terrace. He gave her a slight nod before turning away self-consciously.

Jane sat back down in the wicker chair and piled her long hair onto the top of her head. Why was it always so hot and muggy in Boston in the summer? She reached for the fashion magazine she had tossed aside earlier. It still didn't interest her. She threw it back on the table and leaned back against the chair. Could she keep her sanity for the rest of the summer until she went back to Canby Hall?

Andy came bustling out of the kitchen with steaming plates of food balanced on her small, strong arms. She was uncomfortably hot from the warmth and humidity of the Chicago air. The restaurant her family owned was packed with the lunchtime rush. Andy welcomed the hectic pace. It didn't give her time to miss Canby Hall so much.

She hadn't been home that long, and she

knew her parents were counting the days with dread when she would leave them again. They hated to see her go, but they knew how much it meant to her, and she loved them even more for understanding.

Andy set the plate of beef Stroganoff in front of the lady with slightly blue-tinged hair. She wrinkled her nose and pushed it away with a disdainful finger. "What's that?"

"Beef Stroganoff, madam."

"Well, I ordered the beef Wellington."

"I'm sorry, madam, I'm certain you said Stroganoff. I wrote it down." Andy pulled her pad from the pocket of her apron and flipped to the lady's order.

"I don't care what you wrote down, young lady. I specifically remembered ordering the Wellington."

"Dear," her husband interjected timidly, "I believe you *did* order the Stroganoff."

She puffed herself up like a toad and said, "I most certainly did not. Don't you tell me what I ordered." She folded her arms and stuck out her lower lip like a spoiled child.

"Why don't you take the chicken Kiev, and I'll have the Stroganoff?" He reached for her plate.

She stopped him with a look. "I don't want your chicken Kiev. I want beef Wellington."

"It's no problem, madam. I'll get you the beef Wellington." Andy went back to the kitchen and put in the order for the Wellington. While she waited, she busied herself checking tables and seating the new customers that had just arrived.

She saw the steaming beef Wellington was ready and went to get it. Andy handed it to the woman. Her husband thanked Andy. What was that nice man doing with someone like her? Andy wondered.

When they had finished, Andy stopped at their table. She began clearing the dishes. "Would you care for anything else?" she asked. "We have some delicious homemade desserts today."

"I think not," the woman said, touching daintily at the corners of her mouth with a napkin. "We'll probably stop by Baskin Robbins for ice cream. They always keep their orders straight."

Andy bit back her anger and handed them the check. How did her parents stand this day after day? The crowd was beginning to thin out. The noon rush was almost over.

Andy went back into the kitchen. Her mother handed her a plate of beef stew. "Take a break while you can, honey," her mother advised. "The crowd will start picking up again in a few hours."

How well she knew. She dipped her fork into the stew. The smell was tantalizing, but she would have traded it in a minute for the glop served in the Canby Hall cafeteria.

CHAPTER TWO

After dinner, October Houston sat in the quiet living room with a book she was pretending to read while she watched her father suck thoughtfully on his pipe, the evening paper spread in front of him. Suddenly, he felt her eyes on him and looked up. "Anything wrong?"

"No."

He went back to his paper, but his mind wasn't focused on the day's events any longer. He had noticed such a change in his daughter since she'd come home, a restlessness that had never been there before. Maybe sending her off to school hadn't been such a good idea.

She seemed to like Canby Hall. She had written him frequently, always mentioning the roommates she had become good friends with. It was a relief to know she was making friends. She was too much like him. She took too well to the solitude of life on a ranch.

After her mother had died, Toby spent very little time around any other females. That's why he had sent her to Canby Hall, hard as it had been for him.

Oh, she'd kicked up her heels at first, but she'd learned to adjust. And now as he stole a glance at his restless young daughter, he wondered if she'd readjust to her life on the ranch.

"Those friends of yours. . . ."

"Jane and Andy?" Her face became more animated than it had been all week.

"What are they doing the rest of the summer?"

"Jane was going to spend some time at their summer house in the Berkshires, and Andy is probably helping out in the family restaurant."

A melancholy settled over Toby as she thought back over the crazy year she'd spent with her roommates and the fun they'd had in Room 407.

"You think either of those girls has ever seen a real live rodeo?" her father asked.

"Probably not."

"Think they'd like to?" He dropped his paper onto his lap.

"What do you mean?"

"Well, the county fair is in two weeks, and aren't you still planning to barrel race? After all, you've been to Boston and you've been

to Chicago. Maybe it's about time they came
out to Texas and see how *you* live."

"Really, Dad? You really mean it? They
can come here?" Toby was on her feet and
across the room in a flash, throwing her arms
around her father's neck, crinkling his paper
between them.

Toby's eyes sparkled as she ran into the
kitchen to call her friends. He could hear
Toby's animated voice in the next room.
What would the sounds of *three* lively girls
be like, he wondered. "What did I just let
myself in for?" he asked aloud.

Andy had just kicked off her shoes and put
her feet up on the chair in the restaurant
kitchen, when her brother Charlie pushed the
door open and stood looming above her like
a giant. His large muscular body was such a
contrast to Andy's petite build. "You got a
phone call," he said.

"I do?"

"It's long distance. You better hurry."

"Who's calling me long distance?" Andy
asked with building interest.

"One of those crazy roommates of yours,
who else?"

She ran to the office and picked up the
phone. "Hello?"

"Hey, stranger. How are things up there?"
Toby drawled.

"Busy. How are things down there?"

"Boring." They both laughed. "I was talking to my dad tonight, and he thought you and Jane might want to see a real live rodeo."

"You're kidding! When?"

"Well, the rodeo's week after next, but the sooner you get out here, the sooner you'll get to see Texas."

"Texas, wow, that would be great! I've wanted to go there forever." A twinge of guilt licked at her conscience when she thought about the noisy, busy crowd they'd had during the dinner rush. Her parents were depending on her help this summer.

Andy hesitated. "Well, I have to ask my folks about this. You know I'd love to come, but I haven't seen much of my family this year, and I know they're counting on my being around for the next month and a half."

"So, what's two weeks? Tell them you'll still have a month before school starts. Oh, please, tell them you just have to come," Toby begged.

"Okay, okay," Andy said with a laugh. I'll tell them I *have* to go, and see what they say."

"Call me back right away," Toby said.

Andy put the phone down and went out to the kitchen. Her mother shoved a platter of ribs into her hand. "Give this to Ted, honey."

"Sure." She went back out into the resaurant and caught Ted's eye.

"Table five," he said, "The man in the blue shirt."

Andy set the ribs down, and he asked for more water. She filled his glass and set the pitcher back on the counter. Someone else signaled to her for more coffee.

It was late by the time they finally left the restaurant. Her baby sister Nancy was already fast asleep, and the baby-sitter wasted no time in getting her things to leave.

"Who was that call from this evening?" her mother wanted to know.

"Toby. She. . . ." Andy looked at her exhausted parents and knew she couldn't leave now.

Her father turned to her. "She what?"

"Oh, nothing. She just thought I might want to go to Texas for a couple weeks and see a rodeo."

Her mother and father exchanged looks, and she knew what they were thinking. She wanted to spare them the agony of having to tell her no. "Of course, it's out of the question right now. You guys really need me at the restaurant this summer."

"Will Jane be going, too?" her mother asked.

"I suppose so."

Her father smiled. "Boy, that would be something to see. Jane riding the range in Texas. It's a shame you'd have to miss that."

"Yeah. Well, I'm tired. I think I'll go on

up to bed." It was late. She'd call Toby in the morning and tell her she couldn't come.

"Seems to me the three musketeers wouldn't be much of a trio if one of them wasn't there," her dad said. Andy stopped on the steps and held her breath. Was he saying what she thought he was?

"Maybe you better call Toby and find out more about this trip, so you'll know what to take with you."

Andy turned and jumped from the stairs. "Oh, Daddy, you're the greatest!" She rushed into his arms. "I'll be here the whole month before school starts, I promise, and I'll work extra hard and make it up to you for letting me go."

She reached out with her free arm and encircled her mother as well. "I love you guys," she said. "You have to be the best parents in the whole world."

Jane sat alone at the huge table in the formal dining room playing with the iced tea in front of her. Her mother and sister Charlotte had taken off somewhere early that morning. She had a vague recollection of them trying to wake her and her telling them she wanted to sleep in. Now she was wishing she had gotten up and gone with them.

The grandfather clock bonged ten times. Jane counted each sound as it rang out in the big, empty town house. Bernice, the family's long-time maid came in from the kitchen. "Telephone, Miss Jane."

"Thank you," Jane said. "Oh, Bernice, would you take this in with you?" She handed the tea to Bernice.

"You didn't drink it. I'll cover it and put it in the refrigerator. You may want it later."

"Okay," Jane said. She went into the hall-way and picked up the phone. "Hello?"

"Jane, is that you?" Toby's voice boomed into her ear.

"It's me. Stop shouting. They've made wonderful advances in the phone service since Bell first invented it."

Toby laughed. "I'm just so excited to talk to you! How would you like to make a trip to the wild West?"

Jane felt her boredom begin to evaporate.

"There's a rodeo coming up in a couple of weeks and it's something you ought to see," Toby said.

"Me? At a rodeo? That would be something to see all right!" Jane laughed. "I'll talk to my mother as soon as she gets back."

Jane hung up the phone and dashed into the kitchen. She grabbed Bernice and danced her around in circles in the large, open kitchen. "Miss Jane, what on earth are you doing?" Bernice was unaccustomed to such emotional outbreaks in the Barrett house.

"I'm going to Texas, Bernice!" Jane cried.

A week later, Jane flew into Chicago and met Andy. They boarded the plane for Lubbock, Texas, while Andy's family waved good-bye. Andy looked back and felt a stab of guilt at leaving them again.

It was still dark out when Toby and her father left for Lubbock. They watched the sunrise as they drove the 213 miles into the city. Toby wanted to be sure to get up early enough to see one Texas sunrise while the girls were there. There was just something about watching that red ball of fire turn the sky to lighter shades of purple and orange, until it exploded into blue brilliance over the vast emptiness of the Texas flatlands. It was almost like seeing the beginning of the universe.

The passengers began to file off the plane while Toby searched each face anxiously looking for Jane or Andy. Finally, she spotted Jane's blonde head as she emerged from the doorway. Andy, who was much shorter, was hidden in the crowd.

Toby began waving frantically. Jane's face lit up when she caught sight of her. The stern-looking man standing behind Toby was looking at Jane with curiosity. Could that be Mr. Houston? He was very tall, and he didn't look as old as her own father did. But he had his hand on Toby's shoulder, so it had to be him. Giving Andy a shove, the girls broke free of the crowd and ran toward Toby.

Mr. Houston watched as the three girls hugged each other. Toby's red curly head stood higher than the other two, with the blonde not too far behind her, and the small black girl only reaching to their chins. They were an odd-looking trio.

Toby broke free and remembered her manners. "This is Andy and Jane," she said. Then she proudly looped her hand through her father's arm. "And this is my dad."

"How do you do, Mr. Houston," Jane said.

"Just call me Bill."

Jane thought his accent seemed much stronger than Toby's.

"Well, we'd better head on down to baggage claim," he said.

The three girls chattered endlessly while they waited for their luggage. There was a male flight attendant on the plane; one thought he was cute, the other thought he was weird. One of them liked the food, the other one didn't. As Bill Houston listened to the three of them talking he wondered what it was about these girls that had built such a strong friendship. Not that the two girls didn't seem nice enough. They were all right, he guessed, but they were so much noisier than he'd expected. Toby had never gone in much for giggling girls and yet to see her now, she looked as happy and silly as the other two.

Jane and Andy sat on the edge of the back seat as they drove through Lubbock. They didn't want to miss a thing. The city was considerably larger than Greenleaf, and Jane was sure they would have some great places to shop. She didn't know how far Rio Verde was, but surely they could run into town at least once or twice.

Mr. Houston pulled the car into the parking lot of a stone building that turned out to be a restaurant. "We'd getter get something to eat before we head back," he said. He was a man of few words, Andy observed. No wonder Toby had been so quiet when she first came to Canby Hall.

They went into the restaurant that had a plank floor and large wooden beams in the ceiling. Big, beautiful ferns hung from macramé hangers, giving the place a homey atmosphere.

They slid into one of the wooden booths and the waitress appeared with big brown menus. "Today's special is chiken fried steak, mashed potatoes, and fried okra," she drawled before she walked away, leaving them to look at the menus.

"I don't believe this," Jane whispered in excitement. "We're really in Texas."

"That's right," Toby agreed. "But you haven't really experienced Texas till you've had yourself a chicken fried steak dinner."

They all ordered the special. It came with homemade biscuits and gravy. All through dinner, the girls kept comparing things to the food at Canby Hall. Bill Houston felt somewhat like an outsider eavesdropping on someone else's conversation. Toby had written about school, but he didn't know it as they did. He couldn't even picture what it might be like and hadn't really tried to. Toby was happy there. That was enough.

After the meal, they turned onto the highway out of Lubbock. Jane settled back into the seat feeling content and pleasantly full. She put her hands on her stomach and said, "If I keep eating like this, I'll gain ten pounds before I leave."

Andy rested her head against the door, a contented smile on her face and she let herself be lulled to sleep by the gentle rocking of the car as it sped toward the Houston ranch. In spite of herself, Jane dozed off, too.

The girls woke up about an hour down the road. "Are we almost there?" Jane asked.

"It's still a ways yet," Toby answered.

Jane leaned forward and looked out the window. It looked so flat. There were funny-looking plants with white puffy things on them. "What are those?" Jane asked.

Bill Houston glanced out the side window. "Marshmallow bushes."

"No kidding!" Jane leaned closer to the

window for a better look. Her suspicions were aroused. "I didn't know marshmallows grew on bushes."

"Yup," Toby's father answered flatly.

Jane wanted to see these marshmallows that grew wild in Texas. "Why don't we stop and pick some?"

"They're not ready yet. They harvest them in another month. They're still hard and bitter. They don't get soft and sweet till they're ripe." A smile was beginning to break on his sober face.

"Jane," Toby said. "Those are cotton plants." Toby looked over at her dad, and he grinned at her.

"I didn't think they were *really* marshmallows." Jane moved back and looked out her window. It seemed odd there was no other traffic on the road. The car sped along the empty highway. Jane looked out and saw small green bushy things sprouting unevenly out of the earth. It was such a contrast to the congested East Coast. Everything was so desolate. They had gone at least a hundred miles and there hadn't even been many farmhouses.

The girls talked, played the radio, and occasionally looked out the window as they drove to Rio Verde. Jane began to wonder just how big Texas really was. If they went too much longer, wouldn't they end up in New Mexico or someplace? The possibility of running into Lubbock for a shopping spree began to fade.

Finally, they spotted an outcropping of buildings. Jane leaned against the back of the front seat. That must be the outskirts of Rio Verde, she thought. Then she saw the little square sign that announced the city limits. That *was* Rio Verde. It looked like there was one general store with a gas station out front, and some kind of diner sitting next to it, and a few houses scattered around the area, but Jane wasn't sure because it went by so fast, she didn't have much of a chance to look it over before it was gone.

She looked over at Andy who must have been having similar thoughts about the town. The two exchanged glances and Jane hoped there would be lots to do on the ranch, because there certainly wasn't anywhere else to spend the next two weeks.

CHAPTER THREE

Jane stared at the old farmhouse rising out of the flat ground. The lawn, safely tucked behind the white fence, was the only green for miles. The two-story house looked like something out of the 1800's with all the decorative woodwork around it. In fact, Jane decided, if it were sitting in Boston or any other decent city, it would be quite a house.

Toby jumped out of the car and opened the door as if she were the chauffeur. "This way, ladies," she said with an elaborate bow. "Welcome to the Rattlesnake Creek section of Rio Verde." Jane and Andy climbed out of the backseat. Mr. Houston opened the trunk, and the girls each took one bag, leaving two of the larger ones for Toby's father.

They climbed the three stairs that led up to the big porch. Under the roof of the porch there was a slight breeze, but it didn't do much to squelch the heat of the Texas sun.

The screen door creaked in protest as Toby pulled it wide open and stood against it, letting everyone pass.

The living room was large and airy. The windows reached up two stories and were draped with long ivory curtains. The hardwood floors were broken up by the braided area rugs that were scattered about.

"This is great," Andy said. "It looks like something right out of *Big Valley*." She moved over to the gun cabinet and looked at the numerous rifles encased behind the glass. "Do you really shoot these?"

"Yep," Mr. Houston said matter-of-factly. It would never occur to him to keep a bunch of guns around just for show.

He went upstairs. Toby motioned to Jane and Andy, and the three of them followed him up the wide staircase. The stairs made a sharp turn and ended in a long hallway. The heat was already making Jane feel light-headed when Mr. Houston continued down the hallway and up another, narrower staircase.

"We're headed to nosebleed territory," Jane whispered to Andy who quickly shushed her.

Finally he set the suitcases down in a cheery little attic room. The wallpaper was white with little purple flowers. The quilts were shades of pinks and lavenders with tiny rosebuds and dainty wildflowers. Jane re-

membered the ugly army blanket stretched
across Toby's bed when she first came to
Canby Hall, and was amazed at the color and
quaintness of the room.

"So this is your room?" Jane said, stepping
further in for a better look around.

"No. It used to be my mother's sewing
room. She made these quilts herself," Toby
said fondly. "No one comes up here much
anymore. But it seemed like a perfect place.
We can make all the noise we want and not
bother anybody up here."

The only anybody around to bother was
Toby's father. Judging from the lack of conversation on the long ride to the ranch, Jane
didn't think he was much of a noisemaker.

"Why don't you guys unpack and we'll
go down and see what Abe cooked up for
dinner."

"Abe?" Jane asked.

"He's our foreman, mostly. But he and my
dad trade off cooking, too. Of course, when
things pick up around here, like during harvest or roundup, Dad hires a cook as part
of the crew. Things are pretty slow right
now, though."

Toby sat on the cot at the end of the long,
narrow room. "I'll sleep here. You guys can
decide who gets which bed."

After unpacking, which didn't take long,
the three of them bounded down the attic
stairs. Mr. Houston looked up from his paper

abruptly as the sound shattered the silence in the old house. Toby stopped at the top of the stairs and leaned over the railing. "What's for dinner?"

"Some sort of Mexican casserole, I think. Abe's nearly got supper ready. Come on down and set the table."

He folded the newspaper and set it on the table beside him. The three of them started down the second staircase with more control. Andy and Jane followed Toby into the kitchen.

It was large and airy with high cabinets on every wall. The table sat in a nook that had curved windows facing out onto what looked like a large vegetable garden. Toby got the plates from the cabinet and handed them to Jane. She took silverware from the drawer and gave it to Andy. The three of them got busy setting the table while Bill Houston and Abe finished getting dinner on the table.

"Toby, get the salad from the refrigerator," her father said. He pulled out a funny-looking round dish with a lid on it and placed it in the center of the table. Everything smelled delicious. Mr. Houston sat down.

Abe wiped his hands on the dish towel he'd tied around his waist like an apron. "What are y'all waiting for?" He scooted his chair out and sat down. "Let's dig in before it gets cold."

Jane discovered the little round dish contained homemade tortillas. They were wonderful. The casserole was hot and a little too spicy for Jane's taste, but the flavor was good.

They finished eating and Toby got up from the table and began gathering dishes. "The food might be better than Canby Hall's, but the service isn't as good. We're the cleanup crew."

Jane and Andy got up to help Toby. Mr. Houston and Abe went out on the porch to smoke their pipes and talk about what needed to be done the next day.

Jane had set the last of the dirty dishes on the counter. She reached out and poked Andy in the ribs. Andy jumped and spun around, tossing soapsuds into Jane's thick golden hair. Jane squealed and reached for the dish cloth. She swiped at Andy's face. Toby stepped in between them just in time to get soaked with a cup of sudsy water Andy had intended for Jane. The three of them were laughing and trying to soak one another when Mr. Houston threw open the kitchen door.

The girls froze; hair hanging loosely, water dripping from their faces. "We were just cleaning up," Toby explained.

Her father nodded. "Could you do it a little more quietly? Abe and I can hardly hear ourselves think out here." The door swung shut behind him, and they looked at each other.

"Maybe we'd better mop this up," Andy said, sopping up the excess water with the dish towel in her hand. Jane pulled a long stream of paper towels from the holder.

"I'll just get this water on the floor here."

Toby knelt down beside her. She took dry paper towels and soaked up the water Jane had missed. "Dad will be glad to know the floors won't need to be mopped this week."

Jane looked over at Toby, and they burst out laughing. Andy began to laugh, too. She slid down the cabinet and sat on the floor between Jane and Toby. She reached out and encircled them and said, "Gosh, it's great to see you guys again."

Toby threw the screen door open wide and stepped boldly onto the old wooden porch. She inhaled deeply and said, "Isn't this great?"

Jane squinted at the bright morning sun. "I don't know, I'm not awake yet. Ask me around noon."

"Come on, Jane," Andy said, giving her a playful shove out the door. "Do you want to sleep your whole vacation away?"

"No, just the normal amount of time. We didn't even go to sleep till after three this morning. Then we have to get up to see the sun rise."

"That's tomorrow. I let you sleep in today. It was almost eight o'clock before we got up."

Toby jumped off the porch. "Come on, we're burning daylight."

"How can anyone have that much energy so early in the morning?" Jane groaned.

Toby went toward the barn. "We can ride the horses if you want, or we can take the jeep."

"I vote for taking the jeep," Jane said.

"Okay." Toby went to the tall barn doors and swung one side open.

"Here, I'll get this one," Andy said. She did as she'd seen Toby do, taking the big old door and pushing it out. The door got caught on a clump of tall grass. "Jane, give me a hand here."

"I'll get it," Toby said. She expertly hoisted the edge of the heavy door and it lifted just enough to clear the grass. Toby then kicked the clump loose with the toe of her boot.

She walked into the old barn. Sun peeked through the cracks in the wood and streaked the air with long fingers of light in which particles of dust danced.

Jane followed Toby and Andy into the barn. She stopped and hopped on one foot while she pulled a long piece of straw from her sandal. "Now you see why I wear boots," Toby said.

"I forgot mine this trip," Jane quipped.

The jeep was parked at the back of the barn. Toby got behind the wheel. "Get in."

Jane got in the front and Andy climbed .

into the back. Toby started up the engine and pulled out of the barn. She drove on the road for a while before taking off across the prairie.

"This is the swimming hole," Toby pointed out.

"Can we go there?" Andy asked.

"Sure. It's free. You can go anytime you want."

"Hot as it is around here, I bet you go every day."

"You think this is warm?" Toby answered, "You ought to stick around for August."

"I'd love to," Jane said, "but my family is taking its trip to the Cape in August."

Toby went on pointing out different points of interest around the ranch. This was it. This was her Texas and she was proud of it. She wanted Andy and Jane to love it as much as she did. Andy sat up on the backseat and held onto the crossbar, taking it all in as they bounced along. Jane held onto whatever she could. The uneasy look on her face gave away the fact that she was certain that Toby was going to bounce them all out on the ground before they got home safely again.

Toby pulled up to a ravine and stopped the jeep. She got out and walked to the edge. Jane, grateful for a rest from all the jolting, climbed out, too, and stretched her cramped legs. She hadn't realized she'd been tensing her muscles so much.

Andy hopped out of the jeep and followed

Toby. The ravine's ragged edge dropped off
to a creek running several feet below them.
Long grass shot out from the steep walls on
either side. Trees grew near the water. Toby
sat down and dangled her feet over the edge.

"What's this?" Andy asked.

"Part of what makes this land so valuable.
Fresh water."

"Is this solid?" Jane asked tapping her foot
gingerly toward the edge of the ravine.

"Sure," Toby said. Jane walked to the edge
and looked over. She swayed a little and sat
down. "You okay?" Toby wondered.

"Fine. Fine," Jane said with an artificial
smile. "I'm just not used to the Texas heat."

"What heat? It's still early. Wait'll about
noon." Toby started absently tossing rocks
into the water below. Andy picked up a
handful of pebbles and began trying to hit
a tree on the opposite bank. Toby got into
the game. Both girls stood up and took turns
throwing rocks across the ravine.

Jane got to her feet. "Here, Jane, you try,"
Andy said, handing her a rock.

"No thanks, you two go ahead. I'll just wait
over here in the jeep."

"I don't think she's having a very good
time," Toby said as she looked over at Jane
who was climbing back into the jeep.

"She will. She just has to get used to it,
that's all."

"We'll head on back to the ranch in

a while and go swimming this afternoon. That'll perk her up," Toby said hopefully.

"I don't know about Jane, but it sounds like fun to me."

Toby got behind the wheel and started out again. Andy leaned forward and yelled to her over the sound of the wind rushing by them, "How do you know where you're going? It all looks the same."

"Not when you get used to it," Toby answered. "There's ways of telling where you are, just like being in a city."

"Great," Jane said. "Drop me off at Neiman's."

Toby glanced over at her and Jane smiled. Toby smiled back at her, then she continued. "See that crop of rocks over there?" Andy nodded. "It's about three miles south of the ranch."

"But how do you know which way is south?"

"I just do." Toby never thought about it before. She'd been riding horses on this land as long as she could remember. The idea of getting lost out here had never occurred to her. The early settlers traveled this land before there was anything on it and they never got lost. Why should she?

CHAPTER
FOUR

Abe looked up abruptly from the chicken he had started to fry when he heard the back door open. Flour spotted his face and coated his wispy hair. "You girls worked up an appetite, yet?" he asked.

"Starving," Toby said. She picked up some black olives and a pickle slice from the relish tray on the counter.

"You'll spoil your dinner," Abe warned.

"Are you kidding?" Jane asked. "I don't know anybody at Canby Hall that could eat like Toby."

"Well, dinner'll be ready in a bit. You just hold off some."

"Okay." Toby sneaked one more dill pickle spear and ducked into the dining room to wait for dinner.

Jane and Andy amused themselves looking at old family albums that were lying on a bookshelf in the living room. Jane turned the page to a picture of a little girl with a halo of red curls, wearing a cowgirl outfit and pointing a gun menacingly toward the camera.

"That's you?" she laughed. "You look like Annie Oakley."

"More like Orphan Annie," Andy said, joining Jane in the laughter. "Look at all those red curls."

"Well, I still have them," Toby said.

"Yeah, but now they're kind of coppery, almost bronze. Here they're so — "

"Red," Jane said.

"Well, if you two are through entertaining yourselves at my expense, we'd better wash up for dinner."

"I'm sorry," Andy said quickly when Toby took the album from her hand. "I was only teasing."

"I know," Toby said. "But around here, dinner's no joking matter and if we don't get there before Daddy and Abe, the only thing left will be the gizzards."

The three girls crowded into the little bathroom off the living room. Andy bent down to wash her hands, enabling Jane to catch a glimpse of herself in the mirror. Her hair hung limply around her face. She made a couple futile attempts to fluff it up by raking her fingers through the sides and letting it fall. But it was no use. It kept falling back just like it was before. Finally, she decided it was a good thing that there were no attractive guys within two hundred miles.

Toby moved toward the door and Jane stepped back, ramming her hip into the door jamb. The bathroom was cramped and not built to hold three people. The house had been built when indoor bathrooms were just being put into houses. For years there was just this one tiny bathroom until Toby's mother had had two more added a few years before she died. Now the little room was just an extra bath that hardly even got used.

The fried chicken was even better than the Mexican casserole they'd had the night before. Abe had made biscuits, mashed potatoes and gravy, and green beans from the garden. Jane was impressed that the rough-looking man sitting across from her could cook like this.

Jane wasn't the only one who was impressed. "Everything tastes delicious," Andy said. "If you ever come to Chicago, you have a job in our restaurant."

"No thanks. Cooking for roundup is bad enough for me."

"That's how Dad and Abe met. He was a cook on a wheat harvest, and he just stayed on."

"I liked Texas just fine, and I liked the ranch even better. 'Sides, I was getting too old to go running all over the country. It was time to settle down."

"We're glad you did," Mr. Houston commented.

"Speaking of Texas, how you girls liking it here?" Abe stretched his long arm across the table to dip his knife in the butter. " 'Scuse my reach."

"I think it's wonderful," Andy said.

"Did Toby take y'all to the north pasture? Got about four thousand head up there."

"We never got that far," Toby said. She was working on a chicken leg, holding it in her hands like an ear of corn and rotating it, while she pulled the tender meat off with her teeth.

"I'd like that. Even with the stockyards right there in Chicago, I've never seen a cow up close."

"There isn't much to see, but I'm fixing to head up there to check the stock in the morning. You're welcome to ride along if you want."

"That sounds like fun," Andy said enthusiastically. "Doesn't that sound like fun, Jane?"

"But you'd better pack a lunch. We probably won't get back till afternoon, and there ain't no McDonald's where we're going."

"When are we leaving?" Andy wanted to know.

"After breakfast."

"Are you going too?" Andy asked Mr. Houston, who had been his usually quiet self during dinner.

"Got some work to do on a haying machine tomorrow. I'll have to miss this one. But you girls ought to get a kick out of it."

"I can hardly wait. Checking the stock on a real Texas ranch." Andy saw visions of the old *Bonanza* reruns with the four of them riding up on horses into a flaming map of Texas. Of course, it didn't occur to her that the burning map was of Nevada, *not* Texas, and neither she nor Jane knew the first thing about riding horses.

"Well, you guys hot enough to try out that swimming hole, yet?" Toby asked after they'd finished eating.

"I am," Andy said.

Jane thought about the murky swimming hole Toby had shown them this morning. "Couldn't we just run through the sprinkler?" she said. "It would cool us off, and we wouldn't have to go as far."

"It's not that far," Toby said.

In spite of Jane's reservations, she got into her swimming suit while Andy and Toby were changing. She wished she had brought something more substantial than the white bikini. Like maybe a suit of armor. Who knew what might be lurking in that water to attack her?

She pulled her thick blonde hair back and put an elastic band around it. Just getting the heavy stuff off her neck made her feel cooler. She stood beneath the ceiling fan in the attic room and let the cool breeze blow over her. What she really wanted to do was lie down on the bed and take a nap, but she didn't feel like she had been a very good guest so far. If Andy and Toby wanted to go swimming, she supposed she could try it. It wouldn't kill her. She hoped.

The three of them piled out of the jeep at the edge of the swimming hole. Jane stepped gingerly out into the tall grass. Toby ran over and took hold of a rope that swung freely from a tree and swung out over the water. The rope brought her back over the ground. Toby used her legs to propel herself even further out over the water before letting go of the rope and splashing into the pool below. A few seconds later, she bobbed to the surface.

"The water's great! What are you waiting for?"

Andy took hold of the rope and feebly swung out a few feet. She held on and rode the rope back to the shore and let go. Toby had swum over to the shore and climbed out of the water. She took hold of the rope. "Here, like this," she said, running backward and gaining speed before she lifted her legs and swung expertly out over the water again.

Toby dropped into the water and the rope swung back to Andy. She grabbed it and put her hands just above the knotted place like Toby had done. She ran backward and lifted her legs just before she swung out over the bank. This time she went much further. She took a deep breath and let go. The water felt cold at first impact, but was refreshing. By the time Andy bobbed to the surface and swam toward shore, she had already gotten used to it.

"Come on, Jane, what are you waiting for?" Andy yelled. "The water feels great!"

"I like to get in a little bit at a time," Jane said. She went to the edge of the water. The sandy bottom was visible for the first few feet, then the water dropped off and she could only see the brown surface of the water.

Jane stepped out of her sandals and tested the water. It was warm at the shallow edge where the sun's rays heated it. She took another step out, and her foot sank in the soft, sandy mud. It squished up between her toes and made murky swirls that enveloped her feet and made them disappear.

Jane watched Andy and Toby splashing and swimming in the middle of the water. Nothing seemed to be bothering them. She took another step forward. Something brushed her leg and she cried out. Toby stopped horsing around and looked over. "What's wrong?"

Jane saw it was just a long piece of grass. She felt silly. "I thought I stepped on some glass or something."

"There's no glass in here," Toby said. She was treading water and making swirling rip-

ples that spread out around her. Were there
alligators in Texas? Jane wondered.

"I'll just get out and check it. You two
go ahead." Jane backed out of the water. She
spread her towel under the same tree that
Toby had sat beneath so many times when
she had ridden out here with Max.

Toby swam to the edge of the water and
got out. She came over to Jane. "Is it cut?"
she asked.

Jane pretended to examine her foot. "No, it
looks all right. I'll just stay here a minute
till it stops stinging."

Toby leaned over for a better look, sprin-
kling Jane with water. "Looks okay to me, but
suit yourself."

She ran over to the rope and took hold of
it again. Jane brushed at the mud that was
quickly drying on the soles of her feet. The
splash caused her to look up momentarily.
She watched Andy and Toby play in the
water. The almost nonexistent breeze did
little to cool Jane off. She envied them. But
still, she couldn't grab hold of that rope and
drop off into who-knew-what.

Tony and Andy made several more swings
from the rope into the water. They asked
Jane to join them the first few times then
finally gave up and forgot about her.

Jane dabbed at the perspiration on her
forehead. She felt something crawling on her
stomach and stifled another scream. It was a

trickle of sweat. She wiped it away in disgust. This was an awful place. Why would anyone want to live here? The heat was unbearable.

She looked at the water as it lapped at the shore. It had been refreshing just putting her feet in. Maybe if she went in very quickly and got wet and got right back out, it wouldn't feel so hot to her.

She got up and walked to the edge again. She did pretty well until she got up to her knees and couldn't see the bottom anymore. She watched Toby dive down and resurface a few seconds later. The idea of submerging her face in that filthy water made her shudder. Still, nothing had gotten Andy or Toby, yet. She stepped further into the water.

Jane kept going, taking a step and waiting, taking a step and waiting, until she was waist-deep in the pond. She put her hands out to either side and made little arcs in the water and watched mesmerized as the swirling water reflected the sun's rays. She almost forgot her fears as she bravely took another step into the water. It *did* feel good, and she wasn't so hot and sticky anymore.

Jane's hand brushed against something that felt soft and pliable. It must have been another shoot of tall grass, she told herself. She wasn't about to scream again.

Then she saw the narrow, muddy, brown body slither by. It wasn't a stick. It was alive! It was a snake. She forgot all about not screaming and let go with a blood-curdling cry and bolted blindly from the water.

Jane ran right into a solid mass that took hold of her, and she shrieked again, feeling a wave of dizziness wash over her, nearly causing her to pass out. Her legs buckled and strong arms enfolded her. She opened her eyes and was looking right into the eyes of a tall, handsome boy wearing a straw cowboy hat pushed back to reveal his smiling face.

Jane tried to pull free of his embrace. "Hold it there, little lady. Can you stand up okay?"

"I am perfectly fine," Jane said, throwing his hands off her arms.

"Well, no need to be embarrassed. Lots of women go weak in the knees around me."

"For your information, it had nothing to do with you. I was nearby bitten by a snake in there." Jane pointed toward the menacing water.

"Was it brown, kind of speckly, about this big?" he asked, making a ring with his thumb and finger about an inch and a half around.

"Yes," Jane said triumphantly.

He nodded his head gravely. "Just like I figured. A water snake."

"Are . . . are they dangerous?" Jane asked.

He nodded again. "Some people have even died from 'em." Jane felt faint again. "Yankees mostly." She looked over at his face. A hint of a smile played at the corners of his mouth. "They see them little bitty things swim by and think all sorts of things about them. Then they just up and have a heart attack and boom!" He snapped his fingers in her startled face. "They're gone."

A hearty laugh broke free and filled the air with its boisterous sound. Toby and Andy were out of the water now, standing next to Jane on the grassy bank.

"What happened?" Toby asked with concern.

"She got attacked by a brown water snake." The boy laughed.

"Those snakes won't hurt you," Toby said in confusion.

"Tell *her* that." He broke into fresh gales of laughter, and Jane furiously pushed him aside and went up where she had spread out her towel. She'd had enough humiliation for one day.

"October Houston," he said, "I haven't seen you since forever. Whoowee, you sure have grown up and filled out some," he said looking her over, closely scrutinizing the one-piece swimsuit that set off her nicely curved figure.

"And I see you still haven't gotten any manners," Toby said. "Maybe your parents ought to send *you* away. For about thirteen years." She walked past him and over to Jane. "You okay?"

"Fine." Jane had pulled a white T-shirt

over her suit and was shaking out her towel.

"This a friend of yours?" he asked, following Toby over to where Jane was standing. Much as Jane didn't like herself for it, she couldn't help staring at him. She'd only glanced into his face for an instant, but it was long enough to see the long dark lashes that softly framed his light green eyes.

"This is Jane Barrett and Andrea Cord," Toby said. "And this is Beau Stockton."

"Beau?" Jane said. Now it was her turn to smile. "Do they really name people that in Texas?"

Beau bristled. "It's a family name, but I doubt a Yankee would understand anything like that."

"Oh, yeah?" Jane said dropping the towel and squaring off with him. "Let me tell you about family names."

"Oh, no," Andy whispered. "Here it comes."

"The Barretts of Boston sailed over on the *Mayflower* while your relatives were probably still sitting around, wherever they're from, trying to figure out what crop to plant next."

"Oh, yeah, Miss High-and-mighty? Well, let me tell *you* something. My great, great, great grandfather fought with Jim Bowie and Davy Crockett at the Alamo."

"Oh, yeah? Well, did he win?" Jane asked sarcastically.

"That was low," Beau said hotly. "What'd

your family do that was so great except maybe get on the right boat one day?"

"My relatives fought in the American revolution. They took part in the Boston Tea Party, and the events that shaped this country's future, that's all."

"This could be a long one," Andy said under her breath to Toby.

"I think you're right," Toby said. She stepped forward. "Well, if you two are through exchanging family histories, we ought to be getting back to the ranch."

Beau went to the tree and untied his horse. He stepped easily up into the saddle. "Good seeing you again, October." He always refused to call Toby by her nickname like everyone else. Mainly just to get under her skin. He was a born tease.

"You, too, Beauregard," Toby said, her voice dripping with a heavy southern accent.

"It was nice to meet you, Andrea, is it?" Beau tipped his hat toward her and Andy nodded. "And nice meeting you, Miss Barrett of Boston," he added sarcastically. "Take care of these Yankees, October," he advised. "Looks like they got a lot to learn about being at home on the range." He turned his horse and rode off without so much as a look back.

CHAPTER FIVE

Toby shook Andy's shoulder and whispered, "Come on, time to get up." Then she moved over to Jane's bed.

Andy leaned up on her elbow and opened her one eye. "It's the middle of the night." She dropped back onto the pillow again.

Jane hardly responded at all, other than to bury her head deeper into the pillow and feign deafness. Toby went to the light switch on the wall and flipped it up. The room was bathed in brightness.

Andy opened her eyes. "Are you nuts?" she asked Toby. "It's still dark out there."

"Thought you wanted to head up to the north pasture with Abe this morning."

"I do," Andy said. "Tell me when it's morning." She turned her back toward the wall and closed her eyes again.

"It *is* morning. It's five o'clock. Abe's leaving right after breakfast."

"When's breakfast?" Andy moaned sleepily.

"Twenty minutes." Toby moved over to Jane's bed and took hold of one end of the sheet and pulled it back away from her. Jane rolled over and glared at Toby. "Come on, Sleeping Beauty. We've got to get going if we don't want to keep Abe waiting."

"You guys go ahead," Jane mumbled sleepily. "I have this splitting headache. I don't think I can handle another whole day in the wilderness right now." She pulled the sheet back up and over her head.

Toby shrugged. "Whatever you want, but I'm headed down to breakfast and anybody who wants to come along better get out of bed."

"I'm getting. I'm getting," Andy said. She sat up and squinted at the light. Her arms reached out in a morning stretch as she opened her mouth to yawn. Andy got to her feet and stumbled out into the hall toward the bathroom.

Toby came back and looked at Jane's sleeping figure on the bed. "You sure you don't want to come?" she asked. Jane pulled her arm out from under the covers and waved it in Toby's direction. Toby turned the light off on her way out.

The kitchen smelled of sausage and bacon frying when Andy and Toby got downstairs.

Much to her surprise, Mr. Houston was cooking breakfast. "Where's Abe?" she asked.

"He's out in the bunkhouse getting stuff rounded up to go. He ought to be in directly."

"Then we'd better dig in and help," Toby said.

"What can I do?" Andy asked.

Mr. Houston watched as the girls went into action, spurred by the anticipation and excitement of the day's big adventure. He even enjoyed the sounds of their enthusiastic chatter. Maybe he was getting used to having them around.

Andy, with all her years of restaurant experience, had the table set, the glasses filled with juice, and the coffee brewing in a matter of minutes. She handed serving plates to Toby's father to fill, which Toby then set on the table.

By the time Abe came in from the bunkhouse, they had set a tantalizing breakfast on the table. "Well, you girls ready to hit the north pasture this morning?" he asked pulling his chair back and sitting down. "Hey, isn't there one missing?"

"Jane's got a headache this morning," Toby said.

"Then it looks like you'll only have to pack lunch for three," he said. "Pass me them eggs, please."

The food disappeared quickly. In spite of

the early hour, Andy found she not only had an appetite, but things tasted real good before the sun came up.

Abe finished eating and pushed his chair back from the table. "I'll see you girls outside in about fifteen minutes."

Andy had expertly cleared the table and begun the dishes in the time it took Toby to bring out the things she was planning to use on the sandwiches for lunch. "Sure wish we had some of that chicken left," Toby said, almost crawling into the refrigerator to look. She gave up and shut the door. "Looks like we'll have to settle for sandwiches."

Both girls busied themselves around the kitchen in order to finish up in time to meet Abe. Andy was excited about the outing. Toby took a piece of paper and a pen from the writing desk near the phone. "I'd better leave a note for Jane. She'll wonder where everybody is when she finally wakes up."

"The way she's sleeping, we may be back before she gets out of bed," Andy said with a laugh.

They opened the back porch door and stepped out into the cool early morning air. A gentle breeze ruffled the leaves of the tall maple trees in the yard. Toby jumped off the porch and headed for the barn. The sky was just turning blue. It was Toby's favorite part of the day.

Andy took in all the scenery as they sped

along toward the north pasture. Toby had gotten in the back of the jeep, allowing Andy to sit up front where she could see more. Abe pointed out things as they went along: an area where they found a lot of Indian arrowheads, which probably indicated some battle was fought there; another spot where an old Spanish cemetery had once been that was little more than crumbling stones now.

They came up onto the north pasture, where cattle dotted the horizon as far as Andy could see. They drove the jeep closer and Andy was amazed at how big they looked close up. The really scary ones were the longhorns with their spiked tusks shooting out up to six feet across.

While Andy marveled at the sight of the cattle roaming free on the open range, Jane was rolling over and showing signs of life back at the ranch. She threw off the sheet and looked at the clock, which read ten-thirty. She leisurely stretched her arms high above her head and thought about how good it felt to sleep in.

Jane slipped her robe around her and went down the stairs. The silent house felt so big and deserted. She pushed open the swinging kitchen door. Jane looked around the deserted kitchen. There was a note propped on the cabinet.

Dear Jane,

We've gone to the north pasture. We'll be back early afternoon. Dad's working in the equipment shed out back if you need anything. Make yourself at home. There's lunch meat in the fridge. Hope you're feeling better.

Toby

Great, Jane thought. She opened the refrigerator. Nothing looked appetizing to her. She shut the door and stepped out onto the back porch. She looked up at the tree above her and watched hopefully for some sign of a breeze. Then Jane sat on the wicker rocker and fanned herself with her hand. Was it always this hot out here? She got up and went back up to the room to lie on the bed beneath the whirring ceiling fan.

By eleven-thirty Jane was really bored. She pulled on a pair of pink shorts and a pink-and-white striped top. She started to step into her white sandals and thought about the long grass and rocks that got caught in them all day yesterday. But worse, she thought about the grasshoppers and other assorted bugs she'd kept running into all over the ranch. Jane pulled on a pair of pink socks and her white tennis shoes instead.

She went down to the kitchen and decided to surprise Mr. Houston with lunch. That would give her something to do. Jane stood before the open refrigerator again, moving things around on the shelves, looking for something she could make, but her experience in the kitchen was limited, to say the least.

The back door opened and Bill Houston stepped inside. "Morning. How's the headache?"

"Gone," Jane said. "I was looking for something to fix us for lunch."

"I'll wash up and give you a hand." He went to the sink and turned on the water. "There's some lunch meat and cheese in that drawer there," he nodded over his shoulder.

Jane pulled the drawer open and found a variety of lunch meats. She pulled them out and set them on the table along with the sliced cheese. Mr. Houston pulled off some paper towels and wiped his hands.

"Let's see what we've got here." He took the bread from the bread box and set it on the table next to the lunch meat. Jane watched as he quickly slapped mayonnaise and mustard onto a slice of bread and then piled a variety of lunch meat on top of it.

"What do you want on yours?" he asked.

"I'll make it." Jane reached over and took one piece of bread and cut it in half. She put one slice of liverwurst and one slice of cheese on the bread, before daintily putting the other half of bread on top.

"That all you're eating?"

"I'm not very hungry," Jane said.

Mr. Houston polished off his sandwich and made another one equal to the first in size. When he had finished that he got up from the table. "You mind putting all this stuff away when you're through? I got to get back out there and finish with that engine. I got it all tore apart, and I better get it back together while I still remember where everything goes."

"No, I'll take care of it."

He nodded and left. Jane sat in the silent house and felt sorry she hadn't gotten up and gone with Toby and Andy. She wondered if they were having fun. She got up from the table, put the things back in the refrigerator, wiped the crumbs off the table, and set the dishes in the sink. There weren't really enough to bother with so she just left them there.

She went into the living room and turned on the TV. All she could find were soap operas, none of which she was interested in. She turned the TV off again and picked up the picture album she'd been looking at the night before last. It wasn't nearly as much fun as it had been when Toby and Andy were there to look at the pictures with her. She set it back on the shelf and decided to go out on the front porch.

For a while Jane sat on the porch swing and rocked herself gently back and forth, creating a little breeze. This was worse than being in Boston. At least there she wasn't getting broiled alive while she sat around being bored.

Jane got up from the swing and went down the porch steps. She walked out the gate and toward the area where there was a knoll a few hundred feet to the north. Maybe if she walked over there she could see Toby and Andy coming back. She was anxious for them to get home.

Out from under the protection of the porch, the sun felt scorching hot. Jane dabbed at her brow and kept walking. Every so often she turned around and reassured herself that she could still see the house. She got to the top of the rise and looked out into nothingness.

Jane heard a thundering noise from behind her. She spun around and saw a rider on a huge horse coming at her. There was nowhere to run. He was between her and the house. If she screamed, could Mr. Houston hear her in the equipment shed?

Her heart slowed down as the horse did. She knew that rider. It was the boy she'd met yesterday, Beau something. He pulled up on the reigns and the horse came to a stop near Jane. Beau pushed his hat back and smiled down at her. Jane listened to the big animal's heavy breathing and forced herself to hold her ground.

"Hey, Boston, don't you know little Yankee girls shouldn't be roaming around out here by themselves? Where's October?"

"*Toby* is in the north pasture with Abe and Andy. Mr. Houston and I are minding the ranch till they get back," Jane said haughtily.

Beau jumped down from his horse. He wiped his brow with his forearm. "Sure is a hot one today. Too bad you don't go in much for swimming." He winked at her. "So, did you meet Toby at that fancy school she goes to back east?"

"Canby Hall? Yes. We're roommates."

Beau chuckled. "I bet that was some first meeting."

Jane thought back to that first day. Toby had wandered in, looking like a cowhand, in jeans and that fringed jacket of hers, and tossed an old army blanket over her bed. Jane was in the midst of decorating the room she expected to live in by herself, in a quaint New England style. In spite of herself, Jane smiled. "I guess it was some meeting at that."

"Hey, you can smile." Beau moved toward her for a closer look. "And nothing's broken, either."

Beau sat down on a big boulder. "I guess we did get off to a bad start yesterday. That isn't like us Southern boys. We're usually real polite."

His green eyes twinkled in the sunlight.

Jane walked over closer to him. He certainly was cute.

"You and Toby the same age?" he asked.

"Yes. We're both going to be juniors next year. How about you?"

"I'll be a senior," he said.

"What are your plans after graduation?" Jane asked.

"My plans? Work on my folk's ranch all summer. Do a little rodeoing, I guess."

"Then you're not planning to go on to college?"

"Oh, sure. I thought you meant *right* after graduation. I'll probably go to Texas Tech. Maybe even look into the University of Texas, but that's clear over in Austin."

"That far?" Jane teased.

"My dad needs me to help out around the ranch. I got two brothers in college right now and if I get too far from home, he won't have anyone to help him."

Jane felt a little embarrassed at her sarcastic remark. She wasn't sure if it was the heat or the nearness of Beau that was making her feel light-headed. She stood up. "Well, I suppose I should be heading back."

Beau got up, too. "You want a lift?" he asked. He whistled for his horse. The horse ambled over to them and Beau got on. He extended his hand toward Jane.

"No, that's okay. I enjoy walking."

"Suit yourself," Beau shrugged. "But watch

out for rattlers." He turned the horse and started to leave.

"Wait!" Jane said more loudly than she'd intended. "Rattlers?"

"Yep. Snakes, about six feet long."

"I *know* what they are. Do they really have them out here?"

"Sure they do. And they'd just love to sink their teeth into those nice, firm calves of yours." He turned around again. "Be seeing ya."

"Maybe I will take a ride," Jane said. She went toward the horse, her fear of the snake far outweighing her fear of the horse. Before each step, she'd scour the ground with her eyes looking for anything that moved.

She felt a flood of relief when Beau's firm hand grabbed her arm and hoisted her onto the horse. She held on tightly to his waist as he spurred the horse and it raced off toward the house.

He slowed the horse down about one hundred feet from the house. "How much longer you planning to stick around?"

"Till after the rodeo next week," Jane answered.

"Then you'll get to see me ride."

"Lucky me. Actually, it was Toby we came to see."

"Toby's okay at barrel riding, I guess, but I'm better at dancing."

"Dancing?"

Beau pulled the horse to a stop in front of the house. "Sure. Didn't Toby tell you about the big barn dance after the rodeo Saturday night?"

"Probably. I don't remember it, though," Jane said. She slid her leg over and jumped off the horse.

"Maybe I'll see you there. That is, if I don't get killed in the rodeo first. Bull riding is a dangerous sport. I might even ask you to dance, providing you know how." He tipped his hat to her. "No need to thank me for the ride," he said before he gently nudged his horse in the ribs and was gone.

In spite of herself, Jane watched him ride away. There was something very exciting about him, even if every other sentence out of his mouth was an insult. Well, she would go to the rodeo all right and probably even go to the dance, but she wasn't sure she'd give Beau the satisfaction of one dance.

Dance. That brought to mind Cary. They had met at a dance where Cary's band had been playing. They'd been going together ever since. What would he think if he knew she was even *thinking* about seeing this egotistical cowboy again? Well, he'd never know, because it was never going to come to anything. Beau just wasn't her type. But then, neither was Cary.

CHAPTER SIX

The early morning jaunt across the ranch wore Toby and Andy out. Shortly after dinner all three girls went up to bed even though it was still early. They got into their pajamas and sat on their beds to talk. It was almost like being back at Canby Hall.

Andy flopped sideways across the bed. "That long jeep ride about beat me to death," she commented. "The ranch is just so much bigger than I ever imagined," she said. "How many acres do you own?"

"Out here we talk in sections," Toby said matter-of-factly.

"Sections?" Jane said.

"Yeah. There are six hundred forty acres in a section and people out here measure by sections cause it's a lot easier than talking in acres."

"Well, it has to be the biggest ranch in the territory," Andy said.

"Not really. Stockton's place is about the same size. Of course, they have a couple oil wells that supplement the family income."

Jane's interest picked up and she looked over at Toby. "Oil wells?"

"Yeah. But with oil prices in a slump right now, they aren't doing as well as they were a few years ago, but they're still doing all right."

"Is there any oil on this land?" Jane asked.

"Don't know. My dad's never let anybody find out. He said he doesn't like the looks of those things messing up the landscape and he doesn't need the money bad enough to put up with looking at them." Toby sat back against the wall and tossed her pillow into the air and caught it again. "Besides a dry hole gets mighty expensive."

"A dry hole?" Andy asked.

"Yeah, you can drill a half-a-million-dollar hole in the ground and come up empty-handed."

"Speaking of Stockton's," Jane interjected, "I ran into Beau today, and he happened to mention something about a dance after the rodeo next week."

"How did you manage to *run* into Beau? They might be the closest ranch around, but it's not like you can just run on over and say 'hi' whenever you feel like it. Their place is probably a good thirty-minute ride from here."

"Maybe he came by to see you. He didn't

say. I was taking a walk and he came riding up."

"I doubt I'm the attraction here. We've grown up living next to each other and the only reason Beau Stockton ever rode over to see me was usually because his brothers weren't home, and there was nobody else around he could irritate."

"Well, he does tend to be a little insulting when he wants to be."

"And even when he doesn't. That's just Beau."

"And I don't care about ever seeing him again, but the dance does sound like fun."

"Oh, yes, it would be fun," Andy said, turning around on the bed and facing Toby. "Are we going to go, Toby?" Andy asked. Everyone knew that Andrea would dance till her feet fell off.

"Sure we are. It's part of the festivities, and we don't plan to miss a thing while you're here."

"What should we wear?" Jane asked.

"I don't imagine you brought your boots and a pair of Wranglers, did you?" Toby knew that Jane probably didn't even *own* a pair of jeans that weren't designer labels, much less any cowboy boots.

"Well, no matter, we can run into the general store in Rio Verde and see if they have anything," Toby said. She laid down on her pillow. "Go ahead and keep talking.

I'm listening, but I'm just gonna rest my eyes a little bit."

Jane turned around to say something to Andy who was already dozing off. She looked over at Toby who was barely conscious. Jane had gotten out of bed less than twelve hours before and she wasn't tired yet. She got up and took a magazine from her suitcase and flipped through the pages.

She thought about what Toby had said. How would she look in a pair of Wranglers and Roper boots? She tried to picture herself square dancing with Beau. She shook the image from her mind. It was too ridiculous to even contemplate.

At breakfast the next morning, Toby announced their plans to run into Rio Verde for a little while. Bill Houston only nodded and continued eating.

He pushed his chair back from the table and said, "Clean up the dishes before you go, huh?" He went to the back door and took his straw hat from the hook. "By the way, pick up some more sugar and flour while you're there. We're getting low."

"Sure, Dad," Toby said. She began clearing the table. Jane and Andy got up to help.

"How far is Rio Verde?" Andy asked.

"About twenty miles. If the road is clear, we can make it in fifteen minutes."

"Road is clear?" Jane asked. "Are you ex-

pecting a traffic backup out here?" Jane
hadn't seen another car since they'd gotten
there.

"Not traffic. Farm machinery. Cattle. All
sorts of things can slow you down."

Jane looked over at Toby in disbelief.
"Cattle?"

"Sure. Ranchers moving their stock from
one area to another. Happens all the time."

"Well, then we'd better get these dishes
done so we can hit the road before some cattle
drive beats us to it."

Actually, the drive to Rio Verde was un-
eventful. They came up on a man driving
some kind of big farm machine that Jane
didn't know the name of, and he pulled
onto the shoulder and let them pass. He
waved as they went by and the girls waved
back to him.

The general store was small and cluttered.
But it probably had to be, in order to stock
all the things that the farmers and ranchers
in the area needed. Obviously, it was too far
to run into Lubbock every week.

Toby headed straight to the back of the
store. There were racks of jeans and western
shirts along the sides and assorted boots hung
on the back wall displaying the various styles.

"Well, what do you think?" Toby asked.

Jane wrinkled her nose in distaste. "I think
I'll stay home."

"Why, if it isn't little Toby Houston."

A cheerful old man emerged from a curtain in the back and came over to where the girls were standing. "My goodness, just look how you've grown."

"Hi, Mr. Holtom," Toby said. "We've come to do some shopping."

"I can always use the business. What're you buying today?"

"These are my roommates from school. This is Jane Barrett and that's Andrea Cord. We're trying to get these Yankees to blend in at the barn dance after the rodeo next week."

"Let's have a look here," Mr. Holtom said. He went to the rack of western shirts and pulled out a plaid of yellow, red, and royal blue. "This might be real pretty on you." He held the shirt up in front of Andy.

Andy was busy scrutinizing the shirts herself. She took a soft yellow one with tiny pink rosebuds from the rack. "I think this is more my style."

"Try it on," Toby encouraged. In spite of Jane's protest, Toby went to work trying to find shirts that Jane might like. She would hold up a plaid and Jane would shake her head. Then she would change to a print and Jane would make a face.

Meanwhile, Andy found her size in the jeans and went into the dressing room. She emerged looking like she had been born in the West.

Jane finally settled on a lavender shirt with white piping. She pulled a pair of jeans from the rack and went in to try them on.

She critically evaluated herself in the mirror. She looked stupid. The jeans were too tight and flared out at the bottom to allow for boots. She was used to a straighter leg. She also didn't care for the way the fitted shirt clung to her.

She stepped out from behind the curtain. "Toby, I think I need a different size."

"I wouldn't change a thing, Boston."

Jane froze at the sound of the now-familiar voice. What was *he* doing here? She looked a mess. She hadn't bothered with makeup before they left. Her hand flew up to her hair. It was tied loosely at the back. She didn't know whether to acknowledge his presence or dash back into the dressing room. Toby helped solve the dilemma.

"It's just the style of that blouse. Here, try this one." Jane quickly snatched the blouse from Toby's hand and went into the dressing room, her face aflame.

"I like that one you have on," Beau called from the other room.

"Why don't you see if they have it in *your* size," Jane suggested.

She put the other blouse on and didn't like it, either. What was the use? She wasn't a cowgirl. This wasn't her style. She'd make do with something she already had, or she'd stay home. She put her own clothes back on and came out carrying the others.

Andy was standing in front of the mirror admiring a pair of cowboy boots. She looked adorable in the same style of jeans that Jane thought made her look too big in the hips. Maybe she needed a figure like Andy's to look good in these things.

"What happened to the jeans?" Beau asked.

"I didn't like them." Jane reached behind him and hung the blouses back on the rack.

"Too bad. They looked good on you. Where's that old pioneer spirit anyway?"

"I'm not a pioneer. I'm a pilgrim. Remember?"

"How could I forget? I imagine those shirts would feel pretty uncomfortable to you. They haven't got near enough starch in the collar."

Before Jane could think of an adequate reply, Beau was walking toward the door. "Just put the pitchfork on Daddy's bill, Mr. Holtom." He turned and tipped his hat. "Ladies."

"The nerve of him," Jane fumed.

"He's nervy alright," Mr. Holtom agreed. "Kid's plum crazy. You ought to see him ride a bull." He chuckled to himself. "Nothing like it. Crazy kid's gonna get his neck broke one of these days."

"We can always hope," Jane said wistfully.

CHAPTER SEVEN

Jane and Andy were sitting on the porch swing, and Toby was perched on the railing. They had just cleaned up the kitchen from lunch and were debating on going back to the swimming hole for the afternoon. Toby was wishing she could think of something more exciting for them to do. Jane and Andy had only been here five days, but Toby had the feeling the girls were getting bored. How could that be? She had lived here all her life and had always founds lots of interesting things to do.

Toby got a great idea and hopped off the railing. "I know! Let's go to that old Indian battleground Abe showed us on the way to the north pasture and look for arrowheads."

"Yeah," Andy said, finding Toby's enthusiasm catching. "What a souvenir that would make."

"Want to, Jane?" Toby asked.

Thinking of nothing better to do and deciding it was definitely preferable to going back to that murky old swimming hole that was infested with snakes and other crawling things, she shrugged. "Why not?"

The girls went inside to change from their sandals into tennis shoes, while Toby went out to check the gas in the jeep. The Houston's had their own gas tank as so many of the farms and ranches in the area did. She pulled up to the pump and was filling the jeep when Jane and Andy came out.

"Pretty convenient, huh?" Andy said. "With both of my brothers driving these days, we sure could use our own gas pump."

Andy got into the back of the jeep and let Jane have the front seat. "I've already seen all this the other day. Go ahead and sit up there."

Toby got behind the wheel and started the engine. She turned onto the dirt track that angled out across the ranch. Jane actually didn't mind the drive. The breeze from the open jeep felt better than the heat that clung to her when she was standing still.

Toby drove quite a ways before pulling to a stop at an area that didn't look much different from anyplace else. She hopped from the jeep. Andy and Jane followed her.

Toby kicked at the ground with the toe of her shoe. "Well, this is it."

Andy imitated Toby's kicking motion and asked, "What do we do now?"

"Start looking."

Jane scrunched her forehead in confusion. "For what?"

"Anything. Mostly arrowheads. They look like pieces of rock. Which they are. But they'll be shaped differently. The Indians used flint and other stones to pound sharp points onto them."

The three girls fanned out and scoured the ground. Jane saw lots of dirt and wild grass and a few pebbles, but no arrowheads. Andy's cry brought her quickly around. "I found one!"

Jane and Toby went to her. Andy had something clutched in her small hand. "Let me see," Toby said, extending her own hand toward Andy's.

Andy put a small pink stone speckled with grey into Toby's outstretched palm. Toby held it up and examined it carefully. "Well?" Andy said.

"It could be. See these marks here?" She pointed to ridges on the edge of the flat rock. "This could have been made by someone."

"Let me see that." Jane took the rock from Toby. She held it in her hand and carefully looked at the edges. It really did look like little marks had been chiseled into the stone. How amazing that she could be holding the same rock that had been used over one hundred years ago by some Indian.

"Here," Jane said and handed the arrowhead back to Andy. "I'm going to check around over here." Jane's interest was piqued. She forgot about the possibility of snakes waiting in ambush. She forgot about the heat. The only thing on her mind was finding an arrowhead of her own to take back to Boston and show her family.

Growing up in Boston, she'd been exposed to historical markers all her life. It was the heart of America's history. But there was something different about this kind of history. Maybe because it wasn't behind a glass window in some museum. It was right here beneath her feet. She was standing in a wilderness that had once been roamed by Comanches and Navajo or Apaches or whatever tribe it was they had in Texas.

Her imagination began to run free. She envisioned herself in long petticoats running blindly across the flat ground while buffaloes thundered behind her. But someone was heading off the stampede. She knew what that someone would look like. He would be tall and wearing a straw cowboy hat on his light-brown curls. His green eyes would twinkle and he would lean from his horse and scoop Jane up into the saddle and say, "Well, Boston, I can see you've gotten yourself into another mess."

The image faded from her mind. Why was she wasting time thinking about Beau when she had Cary back home? Loyal Cary. He was enough of a handful with his hair that was a little too long for her taste and the pierced earring that raised her parents' eyebrows. What would her parents think if she introduced them to Beau?

Jane's toe struck something sticking out of the ground. Even with her tennis shoes on, it hurt. She yelped and dropped to one knee. She massaged her toe and looked more closely at the milky stone that was embedded into the dirt. She tried to work it loose by jiggling it back and forth, but it wouldn't budge.

Toby came up behind her. "What's wrong?"

"I stubbed my toe on that thing." Jane kicked the point of the stone that was still partially buried in the earth. "What is it?"

Toby knelt down for a better look. Then she began digging at the dirt around it with her fingers. The hard-packed ground wasn't giving way easily. She did manage to get enough loose to expose more of the flat rock. She wiggled it as Jane had done and more ground broke free. Finally, Toby lifted the rock from its burial place.

Its pointed shape resembled Andy's arrowhead, but it was much bigger. "Do you know what this is?" Toby asked with excitement.

Jane looked at the four-inch rock in Toby's

hand and had no idea what it could be. "An arrowhead for the Jolly Green Giant."

Toby grinned. She looked over at Andy who had joined them. "Better than that. It's a spearhead."

"No kidding?" Jane reached her hand out and took it from Toby. A spearhead. And she had found it. She turned it over in her hands. The marks they had used to chisel the point were much more evident on the larger rock. Jane traced them with the tip of her finger. She wondered if it had ever been used to kill a buffalo or even another person. She shuddered.

Toby was amazed at Jane's luck. "Do you know how rare these are?"

"Maybe I shouldn't keep it," Jane said, feeling guilt and disappointment at having to surrender her treasure.

"Of course you should keep it. You found it, didn't you?"

"But it *is* your ranch."

"Yeah, but that's not my spearhead. At least not anymore, if you want to keep it."

Jane broke into a smile of relief. "Thanks, Toby. This is so cool. Just wait till I show my family. They'll never believe it."

They spent another thirty minutes kicking around in the dirt looking for anything of value. They picked up and discarded several different things that turned out to be just rocks. No one found anything else of interest and Toby could tell by the position of the sun in the sky it was time to head back.

The girls piled into the jeep, each of them submerged in her own thoughts. Jane and Andy clutched the pieces of the past they had unearthed, while Toby stole glances at them and felt content that she had been able to share something special with friends who were special to her.

Jane's find was the topic of discussion at supper that evening. Mr. Houston noticed it was the most excitement he had seen Jane demonstrate since she'd arrived.

"I can't wait to show my family," Jane was saying. "They'll never believe I actually went out into the wilderness and hunted for Indian artifacts."

"Well, it isn't exactly like this is untamed territory," Abe said with a chuckle.

"No, of course not, but you'd never find anything like this just lying around on the ground back east."

"Speaking of lying on the ground, how do you two feel about a little camp-out?" Toby asked.

"Camp-out?" Andy said. Her eyes lit up. "That sounds like fun."

"Camp-out?" Jane repeated. "Like sleep on the ground?"

"Well, not necessarily on the ground. We have air mattresses and Dad has an old army cot around here someplace, don't you, Dad?"

"I think I still do."

"It's plenty warm out. You can lie there and look at the stars above you and listen to the night sounds of the prairie." Toby's mind wandered to the solitude of sleeping out in the open.

"Let's do it," Andy begged Jane. "Just wait till we get back to school and tell everyone. They'll never believe it."

Maybe it was the excitement of the scouting expedition to the Indian campground earlier in the day, or maybe it was Jane's effort to be a good sport. She wasn't sure what the motivation was, but she heard herself say, "Well, okay."

Toby bolted down the rest of her dinner and squirmed anxiously while Jane and Andy finished eating. Andy couldn't help but notice Toby's antsy behavior. "Why don't you guys go ahead and get things ready, and I'll do these dishes."

"Great," Toby said jumping up from the table with no argument. "Dad, do you remember where that army cot was the last time you saw it?"

"Let me see," he said, getting up from the table and following Toby into the next room.

Abe struck a match on the table, set it to his pipe, and chuckled. "I never saw anybody so excited about sleeping on the ground."

Andy looked over at him. "Don't you like camping out?" she asked.

"Oh, I used to, I suppose, but I've spent one too many nights on that hard ground to get too worked up over it now. I just as soon lay my head on a soft pillow." He pushed his chair back from the table and got up. "Be seeing you."

Toby bounded back into the kitchen just as Andy finished up. "Jane's up getting changed. You going like that?" She looked at Andy's tan shorts and cotton blouse.

"What should I wear?"

"You bring a sweatsuit?"

Andrea nodded.

"Then you'll probably want to wear that." Toby started out of the kitchen and Andy followed her.

The three of them came back downstairs. Andy and Jane were in sweats and Toby was wearing her usual jeans. Bill Houston was just finishing putting the sleeping bags and gear into the jeep.

"Where you girls going?" he asked.

"Up on the ridge." Toby said.

Jane looked at the soft green grass around the house and the minimal protection of the fence around the yard and the even greater protection of the house within running distance. "Why don't we just sleep here?"

"Are you kidding?" Toby scoffed. "That's

not camping out." She hopped into the jeep. "Come on, you guys."

The sun was just going down. Toby drove toward the ridge Jane had walked to the other day when Beau had ridden over to the ranch. Jane looked back and saw the lights of the house fading into the distance. The jeep dipped into a valley and the ranch house disappeared from view. They topped another ridge and Jane could still see the house, though it appeared much smaller and further away now. Toby pulled to a stop.

She jumped out and began unloading things. "Let's get this done before it gets any darker." She found a Coleman lantern and lit it. It flared up and burned brightly, filling the campsite with light and casting eerie shadows on the scrubby brush around them.

Toby plugged the air compressor into the cigarette lighter in the jeep and began filling the air mattresses. "Why don't you guys check that area for any big rocks? Just throw them off to the side. When I get done here, we'll start a fire and roast some marshmallows."

"This reminds me of my old Girl Scout days," Andy said as she hefted a good-sized rock and dropped it off to the side. "How about you, Jane, were you ever a Girl Scout?"

"No, I took ballroom dancing at Miss Emily's School that year, I think," Jane said "This is my first real camping trip."

"You're in for some adventure." Toby dropped the air mattresses on the cleared ground and began setting up the army cot.

When they finally had the sleeping bags rolled out and the camp fire going, Toby suggested they sing camp songs. Jane didn't know any camp songs, so Andy and Toby taught her some. She kept readjusting herself around the fire, but the smoke seemed to follow her.

After consuming numerous blackened marshmallows, the girls laid down on their sleeping bags and looked at the blanket of stars above their heads. "This is beautiful," Andy said. "It makes you feel like you're the only person on earth."

"Yep," Toby agreed. Jane had an uneasy feeling, leaned up on one elbow, and reassured herself that she could still see the faint glow of the lights from the house off in the distance. Then she laid back down.

Andy popped up in her sleeping bag and the faint light of the dying camp fire danced in shadows across her face. "Let's tell ghost stories."

"I can tell you real stories," Toby said sitting up in her sleeping bag as well. "Legends about people and places around here."

Toby began to talk in a soft airy voice and Jane wanted to bury her head beneath the pillow. She was having enough problems with this sleeping out stuff without hearing any "Texas Tales."

In spite of her efforts to block it out, Jane could still hear Toby telling about the old woman who lived alone in a small soddy near the Indian burial grounds a few miles from where they'd been today.

"One day she stumbled across a stake half buried in the ground. She worked it loose. It was a broken tomahawk. She took it back to the house with her, thinking if she put a new handle on it, it could be useful.

"What she didn't realize was the tomahawk had belonged to a great war chief who was killed in battle when a bullet tore into the major artery in his thigh and he bled to death. An animal had dragged the tomahawk from the burial site. The chief had been a great hunter and his spirit needed that tomahawk to enter the next world." Toby paused dramatically.

"Late that night, the woman heard scraping sounds outside the cabin door, like someone was dragging something very heavy. She took her rifle and went to the window of the soddy. She couldn't see anyone. The dog started to bark. Someone began knocking at the door. The moonlight illuminated the ground outside her window, and there were no shadows, but the knocking continued."

Toby began to tap a stick against a rock near the fire. Andy's eyes were riveted to Toby's face in the dark. Even Jane had been drawn into the story.

"The old woman moved closer to the door. Suddenly, the dog gave a yelp and stopped barking. The woman shouted, 'Who's there?' The knocking became louder. She stepped closer to the door, the rifle pointing toward the menace on the other side. The door burst open, knocking the rifle from her hands. At first she didn't see anyone there. In her terror, she scrambled across the floor and grabbed at the broken tomahawk.

"Just as her hands closed around it, she felt an icy coldness envelope her. That's when he appeared to her. A dead war chief dragging a useless leg and reaching out for the broken tomahawk the woman threatened to use against him. She tried to scream, but no sound came from her mouth.

"Some men came upon the cabin a few days later. The dog was lying dead near the door, but they couldn't find a mark on him. The old woman was sitting on the floor, the tomahawk clutched tightly in her hands. Her mouth was frozen in a silent scream and her hair had turned white.

"They dug a hole not far from the Indian burial ground. They couldn't remove the tomahawk from her rigid fingers so they buried it with her. They laid the dog at her side and covered the two of them up. People say that when the wind is just right, you can hear a terrified dog barking in the distance followed by a scraping sound as the old warrior tries to pry the tomahawk from the old woman's hands. Then there's always a blood-curdling scream that stops short in the night."

Toby laid back on her pillow knowing that she'd probably succeeded in sufficiently scaring all three of them half to death. Actually, there was no such legend. Toby had made the whole thing up. But Jane and Andy didn't know that.

Long after Toby's steady breathing told Jane she was sound asleep, Jane was listening for sounds in the dark. What if the spearhead she had found belonged to an Indian chief who came looking for it? The thought terrified her. She looked over at Andy's sleeping body. Why had she let these two talk her into this?

Toby would have been happy to know that Jane got to see a Texas sunrise, for it wasn't until the sun came up that morning that Jane finally allowed herself to close her eyes and drift into a fitful sleep.

CHAPTER EIGHT

It seemed as if Jane had just surrendered to sleep when the sound of Toby's voice came crashing into her unconscious mind. She looked out from the protective cover of the sleeping bag and saw Toby's tall, lanky frame outlined in the early morning sunlight. Jane rolled back over and wished for sleep, but the cot was uncomfortable, her head ached too badly, and her eye sockets felt like gritty sand.

She pulled herself up to a sitting position. Andy was already busying herself over the open camp fire. "Better roll out of it or you'll miss breakfast." She snagged the sizzling bacon with the fork in her hand and expertly flipped it over.

Jane was so exhausted, the smell of food was almost nauseating. She laid back down. "You eat. My stomach hasn't woken up yet."

Andy ignored Jane's comment and went

ahead cooking enough for the three of them. She knew once everything was ready, Jane would probably change her mind and be willing to eat.

Toby hunkered down next to Andy. "Smells delicious. I usually end up with a cup of tea and cold biscuits out here when I'm by myself."

Andy dropped the eggs into the hot bacon grease and watched the color go from clear liquid to a milky white. She gently rocked the pan from side to side while she waited for the yolk to cook. She turned to Toby, whose mouth was watering at the sight of the food. "Hand me the plates."

Jane sat up again and pushed her hair back from her face. Her hand held a knot of tangles on top of her head while it rested on her knee, keeping her head in an upright position.

"Still not eating?" Andy asked, looking over at her.

Jane ran her tongue across her lips. There was a gritty taste in her mouth. "A cup of tea would be nice."

Andy poured the hot water into the thick mug and handed it to Jane. "Careful, it's hot."

Jane blew on the steaming liquid and gingerly touched it to her lips. It was hot, but it was just what she needed. As she drained the last of the contents from the cup, she began to feel like she might live through the day. She climbed out from the sleeping bag and went over near the fire. "Got any food left?"

Andy winked at Toby before she took the unused plate and filled it with bacon strips and fried eggs. Jane sat on a boulder, her hair uncharacteristically messy, her clothes disheveled, and it was all Toby and Andy could do not to laugh. Unaware of their stares Jane continued to eat. She cleaned the plate and would have had more if there had been any. Where had her appetite come from? She thought she was too tired to breathe, much less eat.

They packed up their gear and drove back to the house. Andy was beginning to feel familiar with the ranch now. She had paid close attention whenever they had gone out and she was starting to see what Toby meant when she said she could find her way around by using the landmarks. It wasn't that tough, really.

Jane dragged through the day on what little energy she could muster from the two hours sleep she'd had the night before. She caught herself dozing in front of the TV that morning. Later in the day, when they went out to the porch to catch the afternoon breeze, it was a struggle to keep her eyes open.

Toby watched as Jane's eyes would glaze over and the lids would begin to droop. The weight of Jane's head would bring it forward and then she would suddenly snap to full consciousness and look around to see if anyone had caught her dozing.

After the third or fourth time of almost conking out, Toby asked casually, "How'd you sleep last night, Jane?"

"Oh, fine," Jane lied with false enthusiasm. "I had a little trouble getting comfortable on that army cot, but once I did get to sleep, I slept like a log."

"You should have tried the air mattress," Andy said. "It was like sleeping on a cloud. Really comfortable."

Right then, Jane would have given anything to be sleeping on a cloud. In fact, she probably could have slept on a rock, she was so tired.

Andy noticed how Jane kept her head propped on her hand during dinner to keep from dropping face-first into her plate. She was sure now that Jane had probably slept very little the night before.

It was just after eight-thirty when Toby suggested they turn in. She wasn't really tired. Sleeping in the fresh air always left her feeling invigorated. Obviously, Jane didn't share Toby's love for the great outdoors.

Jane pulled her tired body up the two flights of stairs and dropped onto the bed still fully clothed. She was aware that Andy had found a scrapbook in one of the drawers of the old sewing table. In spite of being tired, she rolled over and leaned up on one elbow.

"Look at this," Andy cried with delight. " 'Mrs. McKee's First Grade, Rio Verde County School District'," Andy read aloud. "Mrs. McKee looks a little like George Washington."

"Let me see that," Jane said.

"She does not," Toby defended. "She was my favorite teacher."

Jane sat up and examined the picture more closely. "She *does* look like Washington!"

Andy moved over and sat next to Jane. "See that square jaw?"

"And the hair," Jane said. "I think it's definitely the hair." Mrs. McKee's snow-white hair was combed back from her forehead and fell in waves to her chin.

"Gimme that!" Toby said, grabbing the book from Jane's lap.

"Can we help it if your first-grade school teacher was a ringer for George Washington?" Andy asked.

Toby's hand found the pillow on Andy's bed, and she swung it in a wide arc, knocking Andy sideways into Jane. Andy jumped off the bed and went for Toby. She yanked the pillow from her hands and pushed it down over Toby's face. Toby's physical size didn't make it much of a match. Jane jumped to Andy's defense just in time to catch Andy after Toby had arched her back and bucked her into the air.

Toby scrambled off the bed and onto the other side. Jane and Andy danced back and forth trying to outmaneuver her. All three girls were laughing hysterically and yelling threats at one another.

Mr. Houston could hear the racket from two floors above him. They had certainly had a burst of energy since dinner. He turned to the sports page of the paper and tried to ignore the turmoil going on over his head.

Andy sprang up onto the bed with catlike agility and readied herself to lunge at Toby. Toby surprised her with a tackle around her legs that brought her down onto the bed. Quickly, Toby straddled Andy and began tickling her while Andy screamed for mercy.

Her kicking feet struck out at the air and landed harmless blows onto the mattress. Jane tried to close in and help Andy, but her feet proved too dangerous to get near.

"Stop kicking," Jane cried. "I'm trying to bring in the reinforcements, but I can't get over there."

Toby, who had pinned Andy's small arms above her head, let go of Andy to push Jane back. Andy swung her arm into the air in an effort to free herself. She felt her hand strike a smarting blow against something, and they all froze when they heard the crash.

Mr. Houston threw the door open and

stood aghast looking at the three of them. "What's going on in here?"

Toby was still frozen above Andy. Jane stood at the side of the bed, looking wide-eyed. Mr. Houston's eyes fell on the broken table lamp.

"Toby, I want to talk to you," he said.

Toby got off the bed and went out into the hall with her father. He moved down the steps and away from the door and Toby followed him, but their voices still carried easily in the stillness of the old house.

"Daddy, I'm sorry if we disturbed you. I guess we got a little carried away. It's just that the girls have seemed so bored since they got here and this is the first time they've really been themselves."

Her father wasn't saying anything as Toby babbled on about the accident. "You're not really upset about that ugly, old lamp, are you? We've had it forever. And it was so repulsive anyway. We can get a better one. I can't believe you'd ever even buy anything that awful in the first place."

"Let me tell you a thing or two about that 'ugly, old lamp,'" her father said. "It was one of the first things your mother and I bought on our honeymoon in Mexico. She was so proud of herself for talking the man into dropping his price to half of what he started out at. She didn't even like the thing, but she thought it was too good a deal to pass up. Then as we went on down the street we found the same lamp for less than what she'd ended up paying for it." A smile touched his face at the memory of it.

"We laughed all the way back to the hotel and your mother said no matter how ugly it was, it would always be a reminder of our first shopping trip together. After several years, she put it up here, but she never could bring herself to get rid of the thing." He shook his head sadly. "You broke a lot more than a lamp tonight, Toby. Some things just can't be replaced."

Her father turned sadly away and started back downstairs. "I didn't know," Toby said feebly to his back.

"I know you didn't." He turned back around to her. "I'm sorry I got so upset tonight. Tell your friends. It's just that I'm not used to so much noise, I guess." He continued his descent to the living room. Toby stood on the stairs, even after she had lost sight of his sagging shoulders. She thought about a man much younger than her father, dashing through the streets of Mexico, laughing with a bright-eyed girl on his arm.

Toby came back up to the room. Jane and Andy were sitting subdued on the bed, guilt radiating from their faces. Andy's eyes were swimming with tears. "Toby, I'm so sorry."

"Hey, it's okay. You didn't know. Heck, *I* didn't know." She went to the floor and began picking up the pieces of the shattered lamp. Andy slid from the bed and helped her. Jane took a shoe box from the waste basket in the corner of the room. "Here."

Carefully, as if they were laying to rest an old friend, Toby and Andy set the pieces into the box. Andy stood up and took the lid from Jane and put it over the broken reminders of her carelessness. Andy set the box in the corner near the basket.

"I'll go down and get the broom to sweep up the rest of this before someone steps on it and gets cut." Toby closed the door behind her.

"I feel just awful," Andy commented. "This was all my fault."

"It wasn't any more your fault than it was Toby's or mine." Jane tried to console Andy.

"Just the same, I wish there was something I could do to make it up to him."

The two of them sat in the silence of their own thoughts until Toby returned with the broom. She swept and reswept the area until she was satisfied there were no shards of glass left on the floor. Toby set the broom in the corner next to the shoe box containing the broken lamp. She'd take care of all of it in the morning.

"Guess we'd better turn in," Toby said, remembering how tired Jane had been all day. She turned out the overhead light. The attic room was bathed in blue moonlight. "He's really a super guy," Toby whispered in the darkness. "He's just not used to lots of people, that's all." Her choked voice betrayed her feelings of sadness.

Andy sat up. "Isn't there anything we can do?" she asked miserably.

"I don't know what it would be. Even if we went to Mexico, I doubt we could find another light as ugly as that one." A giggle bubbled up from Toby, and she surprised them all with the sound of it.

Jane smiled, too. "It *was* pretty awful."

Andy suddenly had a great idea. "Look, since we got here, we've made more work for your dad. We haven't really done anything to help out, right?"

"What could you have done?" Toby asked, leaning up on her elbow and looking across the moonlit room at Andy's animated face.

"Well, I can cook. I've watched my mom in the restaurant for ages, and I know how to make a pretty decent meal if you have all the right stuff. Why don't the three of us make a really special dinner for him tomorrow night?"

"That's a great idea," Jane said. "We can set the table in the dining room and eat by candlelight and make it a dinner to remember. What do you think?"

"I think it sounds wonderful!" Toby said.

She was disappointed her dad hadn't gotten to see the best side of Andy and Jane. Maybe this was just what he needed.

The girls all retreated to their own thoughts. The steady breathing in the room was proof that none of them would have trouble sleeping that night.

CHAPTER NINE

Unable to sleep very well the night before, Bill Houston had gotten up early and gone out to mend some sagging fence posts. As he pounded the posts back into the ground, his mind continued to replay the confrontation scene of the night before.

He should have handled it differently. Toby had no way of knowing what that old lamp had meant to him. He should have packed it away years ago. He thought about the expression he had seen on Jane and Andy's faces when he'd burst into the room. What were they thinking now?

He just wasn't used to kids. At least not so many of them. Nor such noisy ones. Even his own daughter had been unusually loud, or so it seemed. She had always been so quiet and content to be by herself. Watching her with these two friends of hers was like seeing a stranger wearing his daughter's face.

He shook his head. Wasn't that what he wanted? Hadn't he sent her away for her own good? He had worried about her inability to get along with other kids. She seemed content to isolate herself on the ranch. Now he had to worry about whether she had changed so much that the isolation of the ranch would be unbearable for her.

He took off his straw hat and ran his forearm across his forehead. The fabric of his cotton shirt absorbed the dampness. He saw a cloud of dust in the distance. It was the jeep. He knew Abe was checking stock near the ridge, so it had to be Toby.

When the girls had gotten up, they had rushed downstairs to tell Mr. Houston of their plans to make him an elegant dinner. He had already left in spite of the fact that the clock in the kitchen read six-fifty.

Toby remembered him mentioning something about working on the fence. She knew right where he would be. After breakfast, the three of them went out to the barn. Andy grabbed Toby by the arm. "Are you sure we should go with you?"

"Why not?"

"Maybe you should go out alone and talk to him."

"Andy, he doesn't bite."

"I know that. I just didn't want to embarrass your dad."

"Look, this was all your idea. I want you there when we tell him about it."

They all piled into the jeep. Toby took off across the parched ground. Jane watched the landscape speeding by. Maybe Toby knew where she was going, but it all looked the same to her. Once she lost sight of the house, she never knew where she was.

Off in the distance, they could see the small figure of Bill Houston. He appeared to grow larger as they got closer. He took his hat off and wiped his face. Then, shadowing his eyes with the large straw hat, he watched them approach.

Toby pulled the jeep to a stop. "Morning," she said.

"How you feeling this morning, ladies?" he asked, before putting his hat back on his head. In spite of the earliness of the day, the heat was already rising. It was going to be a hot one.

"We feel terrific 'cause we have this great idea," Toby said. "Actually, it's Andy's great idea." Toby looked over at Andy.

"What's that?" he asked.

"We figured you might like the night off. It might be nice to just come in and relax," Toby said.

"So, we thought it would be nice if we fixed dinner for you and Abe tonight," Andy said.

Mr. Houston grinned. "That'd be pretty

nice alright, but Toby here isn't much of a cook."

"But that's where I'd come in," Andy told him as she got out of the jeep. "I've watched my mother cook since I can remember. I know my way around a kitchen as well as Toby knows her way around this ranch."

"Oh, you do, huh?" An amused smile was on his face.

"So, how about it, Dad? Let us take care of you for a change. Take the night off. Relax. And you won't even have to do the dishes."

"That's right. We'll do it all," Andy said. "Our treat."

"Ladies, that sounds too tempting to pass up. My mouth is watering already."

"Well, don't get too excited. It'll take us most of the day to get things ready. We have to run into Rio Verde for a few supplies, but we'll be back around noon." He nodded. "You're gonna love it, Dad. Just wait and see."

Toby's eyes sparkled as she looked over and smiled at him. Andy and Jane seemed much more relaxed, too. He knew this was their way of apologizing and he appreciated it. Tonight after dinner he would make a little apology himself.

Back at the ranch, Jane and Andy scoured the shelves of the pantry, checking to see what they would need to buy, while Toby looked through the freezer to see what cuts of meat were left. They were due to slaughter a cow in about a month or so, right after roundup. Right now it was pretty slim pickings.

Andy went out to the little room off the back of the kitchen. Toby was almost standing on her head in the old chest freezer throwing things from one side to the other after she'd read the labels on the frozen meat.

"Find anything?" Andy asked.

Toby almost tumbled headfirst into the frozen beef. She turned and stood up to face Andy. "Hamburger, pot roast, ribs," she shrugged. "There's chicken, but that's about it."

"I can make barbecued ribs," Andy said enthusiastically.

"You can?" Jane asked in wonder.

"Well, I've never actually made them before, but I've watched my mother, and I'm sure I could do it. Do you guys have any cookbooks?"

"I think there's some out in a drawer in the kitchen." Toby shut the freezer and led the way. "Here," she said, producing a well-worn cookbook whose pages were falling out.

Andy sat on the chair and flipped the book open to the table of contents. She looked up sauces and barbecue. The contents said she should turn to page 113. She flipped through the book and found it jumped from page 97 to 121. She double-checked the table of contents, then slowly looked back through the book. There was no page 113.

"That's okay," she said, closing the book and standing up. "I think I can remember how she does it."

Jane eyed her suspiciously. "Are you sure about this?"

"Of course, I am," Andy said. "Have you got that shopping list we made up?"

Jane waved the paper in the air. "Right here."

"Then let's get the shopping done. We've got a lot to do before tonight."

Toby grabbed the keys to the jeep and the three girls piled out the back door, nearly running each other over in their excitement to get into Rio Verde. They wanted to hurry back and get on with the adventure of preparing a candlelight dinner that would long be remembered.

In the small grocery store, Toby squinted at Jane's quickly scribbled writing as she tried to make out the name of the spice Jane had written down. "What is this?"

Jane studied the paper a minute. It had been difficult for her to write, as she was balancing on one foot while using her other leg as a writing table. "Looks like Cheyenne pepper."

"Cheyenne pepper?" Toby repeated.

"I think that's what she said."

Toby went over to Andy. "What's Cheyenne pepper?"

"Cheyenne pepper?" She took the list from Jane's outstretched hand. "That's cayenne pepper," she corrected.

"I was close," Jane said.

Toby and Jane went back to the spice rack. They couldn't find any cayenne pepper. Jane picked up a metal can that read chili pepper. "What about this?"

"One pepper is probably like another," Toby shrugged. "We'll just get that."

Andy had had to make some substitutions herself. Spices and ingredients that she was used to seeing her mother use weren't available in the little store. She was almost certain that the substitutes would do the job equally as well.

"Well, that's everything," Andy said. "We'll have a feast fit for a king tonight."

"Oh, wait!" Jane cried. She went down the aisle she'd spotted earlier and got the long blue candles. "Do you have any holders for these?"

"I'm sure we do someplace," Toby said. "But, Jane, why blue ones? Wouldn't some other color be better?"

"Maybe, but this is my favorite color."

It was after lunch when Andy tied a towel around her slim waist and turned to her helpers. "The first thing we have to do is bake the pies and start the bread so the dough has time to rise."

Andy set to work immediately calling out supplies that Toby would locate and bring to her. She expertly kneaded the lump of dough with her capable hands. Jane watched in amazement as Andy was transforming into a chef right before her eyes.

She put the dough into a greased bowl and covered it to let it rise. Then she began mixing the dough for the pie crust. "While I'm doing this," she said to Toby, "you peel the apples."

"What can I do?" Jane said, anxious to help.

"Turn the oven on to four hundred degrees and then see if you can find those candle holders."

Andy rolled out the near perfect crust and began slicing apples that Toby had peeled. She put them on top of the layer of pie crust. She read the recipe for apple pie from one of the loose pages in the cookbook Toby had found for her. She sprinkled various spices into the pie. In her rush to get the pie in the oven before the bread got too high, she accidentally grabbed chili powder instead of cinnamon. She sprinkled in the teaspoon on top of the other spices and mixed it all carefully.

After laying the top layer of pie dough on the pie and pinching the sides together, she set it in the oven. The bread dough was well above the top of the bowl. Andy carefully punched it down, bringing the sides gently toward the middle like she'd seen her mother do a dozen times.

"Got any loaf pans?" she asked Toby.

"I'm sure they're around here somewhere." Toby kneeled down and looked through the big cupboard that contained all the cooking pans.

"Look what I found!" Jane cried.

Toby jerked her head around and bumped it on the cabinet. "Ow!" she yelped. Rubbing her head she climbed back out to have a look at what had Jane so excited.

Jane was holding cut crystal candle holders. Toby remembered seeing them on special holidays years ago when they would have dinner in the formal dining room.

She turned and sat on the floor. "I'd forgotten we had those."

"Is it okay to use them?" Jane wanted to know.

"Sure," Toby shrugged. "I don't know why not." She pulled the loaf pans from the shelf and extended them up to Andy. "Here. These what you wanted?"

"Perfect," Andy said. She set Toby to work greasing and flouring the pans while she shaped the dough into loaves. She wished she'd paid closer attention to that part. She kept coming up with a seam on the side or the top, or having one loaf a lot bigger than the other.

Finally, she rolled it into a log and pinched the sides underneath. It looked like a loaf. She covered the loaf pans. "Now, we just have to wait for the bread to rise while that pie finishes cooking."

Toby looked at the bubbling apple pie through the glass of the oven door. "It looks great." She pulled the oven open and caught a whiff of it. It smelled pretty good, but there seemed to be an extra odor that she couldn't put her finger on. She shrugged and closed the oven door.

Andy was trying to remember all the ingredients her mother used in her barbecue sauce, when the timer went off signaling the pie was ready. She opened the door and saw the golden crust. She reached for the hot pads and lifted it carefully from the oven and set it on a cooling rack.

She took the loaves of bread and slid them into the oven. She looked over at Jane and Toby. "So far, so good. There isn't much more we can do for a while, till that bread comes out of the oven."

The three of them sat around the table looking at each other. "This might not make up for last night," Jane said, "but it sure does bring back memories of last Christmas vacation when we all ended up working in your family's restaurant."

"I just wish we could do more," Andy sighed. Then her face lit up. "Do you have any glue around here?"

"Probably."

"Well, where?" Andy insisted. Toby got up and went to the desk. She pulled out drawers and moved papers around and finally retrieved a small bottle of white glue.

"Ta da!" she cried. "Now what?"

"Now we put that busted lamp back together," Andy explained. "It may not look as good as new, but we have all the pieces and we might as well try."

"It'll be something like fitting the pieces of a jigsaw puzzle together without a picture, won't it?" Jane wondered.

"You wait here and let me know if Toby's dad comes back. In the meantime watch the bread and take it out when the top turns to golden brown. We'll go up and see about repairing the lamp. Then we can give it to him after dinner as a really special surprise."

The two of them dashed upstairs, inspired by their latest brainstorm. Jane sat down at the table and flipped through the pages of the dilapidated cookbook. She got up and looked at the bread in the oven. It hadn't even begun to turn yet.

The oven was doing its best to heat up the kitchen. Jane fanned herself with one of the pages that had fallen onto the table from the deteriorating cookbook. It was little relief.

She stepped out onto the back porch and stood in the doorway where she would be sure to hear the timer. There was a slight breeze that cooled her face as it blew across her.

Leaning back against the door jamb, she lifted her hair into a pile and held it on her head, while she continued to fan herself with the page she held in her other hand. She kept the door propped open with her outstretched foot.

"Warm enough for you, Boston?"

Jane's eyes flew open at the sound of the familiar voice. She saw Beau standing at the bottom of the steps, his wide grin spreading across his face. "You ought to take a dip in the swimming hole."

She dropped her hair and wondered how bad she must look. "I was out riding and since I was in the neighborhood, I decided to drop in."

"I didn't hear you come up," Jane stammered.

"I rode up out front. I knocked on the door. No one answered so I walked around back here to see what was going on." He stepped up onto the porch, swung his leg up onto the railing, and sat down.

Jane let go of the door and came out to sit in the wicker rocker near him. What was it about this guy that she found so attractive?

"So what you been up to since the last time I saw you?" he asked.

"Just the usual things. Exploring. Camping out."

He threw his head back and laughed. "You? Camping out?" He noticed the angry look on Jane's face. "I'm sorry. I just can't imagine you out there getting next to nature."

"Well, I did. And I must admit, it was a wonderful experience," Jane lied.

He tried to hide his grin. "I'll bet it was. Toby *did* have you shake out your shoes in the morning, didn't she?"

"Whatever for?"

"Scorpions."

Jane rolled her eyes skyward. "Save it. We didn't shake out anything and nothing attacked us during the night." Just the same Jane was glad the camp-out was behind her. If she had known about the scorpions, she would have never gone to sleep at all.

"That was lucky," Beau said.

"You know, you are really amazing. Have you ever been in New York or Boston?" Jane asked.

"No."

"Have you ever been any further east than Dallas?"

"Well, no."

"That's what I thought. It's so easy to sit there and feel superior when you've never been anywhere else, but I will tell you this much, Mr. Stockton, a midnight ride on the New York subway system would rival anything you have out here for thrills and danger."

"You're probably right." He moved over and sat on the chair beside her. "Why don't you tell me about it."

Toby and Andy struggled to fit in the piece they knew had to belong in the jagged opening they had left. One jutting little corner kept the whole thing from sliding easily into place.

"Let me see that," Toby said. She took the lamp and screwed her face into a mask of concentration as she gently tried working the piece back and forth into the hole.

"Be careful with it," Andy warned. "It's not completely dry, yet."

Putting the lamp together had turned out to be a monumental chore. The glue wasn't drying as quickly as they thought it would and between each piece they had to blow on the surface and fan the lamp to help speed up the process. Luckily, the lamp had broken into several large pieces.

Toby gave the stubborn piece one good shove. The chip broke off and the piece settled into place at a somewhat imperfect angle. She carefully held the lamp up for inspection. "What do you think?"

Andy looked at the crisscrossing seams and the globs of clear white glue that were almost dry. "Well, no one can say it's a perfect job," she commented.

"Guess it'll be kind of obvious it was broken once, huh?"

"Yeah, maybe we should just forget it."

"Let's just set it over here in the corner and let it dry. We'll see what Jane thinks."

"Speaking of Jane, I wonder how she's doing down there," Andy said as she got up off her knees and stretched. They had been working on the lamp for over an hour. "We'd better get down there or I'll never have dinner ready on time."

They smelled the burning bread at the top of the second floor. Toby and Andy exchanged looks and shot down into the kitchen. The smell grew more pungent when they opened the kitchen door.

Toby threw open the oven and the tops of the perfectly shaped bread were blackened and charred. Grabbing a hot pad, Andy moved Toby aside and reached in for the loaf pans. "Get me a cooling rack," she ordered. "Hurry."

Toby slid the apple pie from its rack and handed the wire cooling rack to Andy. Andy expertly flipped the loaf of bread onto the metal rungs, hoping only the top had burned, but the loaf was evenly blackened on all sides.

"Where's Jane?" Andy fumed. "She was supposed to be watching the bread."

"Jane?" Toby called. There was no answer. She went into the living room, thinking Jane had laid down to rest and fallen asleep. She didn't see her, but she did see the big bay outside the window. It was Beau Stockton's horse. She went out the front door and looked for them. She couldn't see them anywhere. She called Jane's name again. There was no answer.

Toby came back into the kitchen. "I can't find her."

Andy looked up at her with worry in her eyes. "Do you think something's happened to her?"

"I'm sure of it," Toby said. "Beau Stockton's horse is out front. Come on." Toby went out the back door with Andy right at her heels.

In the distance, she saw Jane and Beau walking back toward the house. Jane saw Toby and Andy and waved to them. Andy didn't return her wave, but rather planted her fists on her hips and glared back at her.

"The bread! Oh, my gosh! I forgot the bread," Jane cried and began running toward the house.

"You're a little late," Andy said.

"Is the bread finished?" Jane asked weakly.

"Yeah, it's finished," Toby said. Beau had caught up with Jane and was standing behind her on the porch.

"What's going on?" he asked breathlessly.

"I was supposed to be watching the bread, and I forgot all about it. I think it might have gotten too done." She went into the kitchen and saw the blackened loaves on the cooling rack.

Beau, Toby, and Andy had followed her into the house. "Guess you won't be having bread this evening," he observed. "Glad I wasn't planning to stay to supper."

"I don't believe you were invited," Toby said.

"You got a point there. Guess I'll just see myself out." He stopped in the kitchen doorway. "Hey, Betty Crocker, I'll see you at the rodeo Saturday."

Jane pulled her eyes away from the burned bread and glared at him. "Don't hold your breath."

"And don't forget to save me a dance Saturday night," he continued, as if he hadn't heard her. He glanced at the blackened bread in front of her. "I sure hope you can dance better than you can cook, Boston." His good-natured wink was wasted on Jane.

Chapter Ten

The Houston's oven was hotter than her mother's. Andy looked at the scorched sides of the barbecued ribs and nearly burst into tears. "Is anything going to be edible?" she asked.

"Don't worry, I'm sure it will all taste better than it looks," Jane said. Andy looked over at her sharply and Jane shrunk back away from her gaze when she realized how bad that sounded.

"Lighten up, Andy," Toby said. "Everything smells delicious. And I know the baked potatoes will be great. It's pretty hard to mess those up." Andy looked from Toby to Jane and then pulled the towel from around her waist and went into the dining room.

"Now you've hurt her feelings," Jane said.

"Me?" Toby cried. "What about you?"

"Okay, we both did. Let's go tell her we're sorry." Jane and Toby followed Andy into the next room. She was sitting at the table. The expression on her face spelled out the certain disaster she felt dinner was sure to become.

Toby sat down next to her. "Hey, what's with this look of impending doom? The ribs smell delicious."

"But they're overcooked. They'll be dry and tough."

"How do you know? I think they smell delicious, too," Jane said.

"Do you really?" Andy turned her hopeful eyes on Jane.

"Yeah, I can hardly wait to eat." All three of the girls had skipped breakfast and eaten a light lunch in order to get on with the big feast.

Toby became aware of the rumblings in her own stomach. "Yeah, don't worry about dinner. I bet everything will taste great. And I'm hungry enough to eat a horse right now."

Jane glared at Toby and Toby smiled at Andy. Had she done it again? Andy smiled back and she seemed much calmer than she had when she'd fled the kitchen.

"Hey, where is everybody? We're starving," Abe called from the kitchen.

"We're in here," Toby answered.

The door opened and Abe and Bill Houston were standing in the doorway. "Is dinner almost ready?" her father asked.

"Whenever you're ready, we can put it on the table," Toby said.

"We'll wash up and be right there," Mr. Houston said.

The three girls went into the kitchen. "Toby, get the relish plate from the fridge," Andy commanded. "Jane you take the baked potatoes and green beans. I'll get the ribs."

Andy began scooping out the ribs and putting them on a serving platter. Much of the barbecue sauce had evaporated and thickened in the overheated oven. Andy scraped out as much as she could, but it was too thick to spread evenly over the ribs. She piled a clumpy spoonful onto the ribs and choked back her tears again.

Toby came back into the kitchen from the dining room. "That everything?"

Andy glanced sadly at the garbage where they'd buried the burnt bread. "Everything that's edible." She picked up the plate of ribs and went into the dining room. Jane was just lighting the candles.

Abe and Bill Houston came into the dining room. Abe rubbed his hands together. "Everything looks mighty tasty."

"It certainly does," Mr. Houston agreed. "The table looks very nice, girls. Even provided us with candlelight." Then his eyes fell on the crystal candle holders. A cloud of sadness seemed to pass over them. Jane shot a worried look at Toby. The three of them waited to see if he was going to say anything.

As quickly as it came, the look of melancholy went away. He pulled his chair back and sat down. "Well, let's eat this while it's hot."

Jane, Andy, and Toby sat down as well. They began passing food around the table. Everyone generously filled his or her plate. Andy glanced around the table and felt pleased. It was the first complete meal she'd ever done. Always before, she'd had her mother nearby for advice and her brothers to share the work. But this meal was all her own doing.

Abe picked up one of the ribs from his plate and tore into it with his teeth. The toughened meat stubbornly clung to the bone and he had to really yank to pull it loose. He set the rib back on his plate and began the monumental task of chewing it.

Bill Houston cut into his baked potato. The knife which should have slid easily into the steaming potato, hit a hard place in the center where the potato was still raw and stopped. He forced it downward and the knife smashed through to the other side causing a loud clanking sound against his plate.

"Is it done?" Andy asked fearfully.

"Crunchy," Bill Houston said. "Just the way I like them."

He smiled at Andy and reached for the butter. Jane and Toby were busy trying to get their own potatoes cut in two. "I believe I'll just have half a potato," Jane said. "They're so fattening, you know."

"I'll split with you," Toby said quickly as she put hers back on the serving plate.

"Why don't you cut it?" Jane said. She was preoccupied with finding some ladylike way to eat the messy ribs. She didn't want to pick them up and tear the meat off with her teeth like Abe and Toby's father had done, but the butter knife at her side wasn't sharp enough to saw through the meat on her plate.

"Could you pass me the green beans?" Abe said.

Andy quickly grabbed the bowl and passed them around the table. "I believe I'll have some more of those, too," Mr. Houston said. They all began piling a second helping of green beans onto their plates. Andy knew why. They were the only things on the whole table fit to eat.

No one was saying anything during dinner. They were all looking at their plates. Occasionally, a fork or a knife would bang loudly against a plate when someone pushed down too hard while trying to cut either the meat or the underdone potato.

"Well, I hope you didn't get too full," Toby said, getting up from her chair and looking at the half-filled plate around the table. "There's apple pie for dessert."

"Hey, now that sounds real good," Abe

said. He handed his plate to Toby. "I believe I better stop right here so I still have some room."

"Me, too," her father said. He extended his plate to Toby.

"I'll get that," Jane said. She took her own plate which she had skillfully covered with her napkin and followed Toby into the kitchen.

"I certainly hope this is edible," Jane whispered. "I'm starving."

"Shhhh," Toby warned. "She'll hear you."

Toby took the golden-brown pie into the dining room. Her father and Abe both looked up and smiled at the welcome sight. "Make mine a big one," Abe said.

"Same here," her father echoed.

Toby handed the pie and the knife to Andy. "Would you like to do the honors. After all, you baked it."

Andy, who had been unusually quiet, took the knife and slipped it into the pie. There was a visible sigh of relief when she realized the apples were done. At least something besides the green beans had turned out right.

She cut generous pieces for Toby's father and Abe. She passed them across the table. Toby looked at the juicy filling that was slowly oozing from the pie. "I'll take one the same size," she pointed out.

"Me, too," Jane echoed.

"What about your diet?" Andy wondered,

but she cut two large pieces and passed them out as well. She took a smaller piece for herself. She had finally given up and pushed the remainder of her own meal away. They would have to fill up on apple pie tonight.

Mr. Houston was the first to bite into the pie. He screwed up his face and gulped hard. Abe took a generous mouthful and almost gagged. He immediately reached for his iced tea and took several gulps.

Andy watched their expressions in puzzlement. What could be wrong with the pie? She'd followed a recipe. It had to be all right.

Jane's fork slithered beneath the crust and dragged one lone apple out. She put it in her mouth and involuntarily made a face. What was in that pie, she wondered?

Toby had been busy mashing her own piece and mixing it all together the way she liked it and hadn't noticed the scene at the table. She scooped up a forkful and popped it into her mouth. It took her tastebuds a minute to register the flavor of the pie. Something was very wrong here.

Andy looked from one startled face to another and finally couldn't stand the suspense any longer. She slipped her own fork into the pie and put it to her mouth. The sweetness of the syrup mixed with the spicy hotness of the chili powder, to create somewhat of a cross between apple pie and an enchilada.

Andy dropped her fork onto her plate and

burst into tears. She ran into the kitchen with Jane and Toby right behind her. Andy was sitting on the back porch in the wicker rocker, weeping.

"I wanted everything to be so special," she sobbed.

"It wasn't that bad," Toby lied.

"Oh, yeah? If you want seconds there's plenty left."

"So maybe you're not ready to fill your mother's shoes, yet," Jane reasoned. "You still have a lot of potential. If I hadn't burned the bread, I'm sure it would have been wonderful."

"It was probably a lucky thing you did burn it. It would have just been something else that wasn't fit to eat."

"Hey," Toby reminded her, "The green beans were great."

Jane elbowed Toby. Then she sat down beside Andy. "Look, you did the best you could. You didn't have a cookbook or your own kitchen to work in. You can't help it things turned out unfit to eat."

Andy pulled her head up sharply. "Why don't both of you just leave me alone?"

"Good idea," Toby said, pulling Jane back toward the kitchen. "We'll just go on in and clean up the kitchen, and you come in whenever you're ready 'cause we'll be right here."

"Yeah," Jane said. "We'll be right in here."

They went back into the house. Abe and

Bill Houston were making peanut butter sandwiches. "Care for one?" Abe asked.

"I'd kill for one," Jane said. "I'm starving." She took the peanut butter and spread it across the bread, then swirled the jelly on top and placed the second slice of bread over it all. She bit into the sandwich and thought never in her life had peanut butter and jelly tasted so good.

Andy had dried her eyes and decided to come back in and help clean up the mess in the kitchen. It was the least she could do. After all, she had made most of it. She went to the back screen door and saw everyone sitting around the kitchen table, laughing and eating peanut butter sandwiches.

Andy turned away from the door as a flood of fresh tears coursed down her face. She ran off the porch and into the night, sobbing blindly as she ran.

Jane and Toby began clearing the table in the dining room and bringing the dishes into the kitchen. Jane picked up the broiling pan that Andy had cooked the ribs in. It was not only greasy, but there was a crust of blackened sauce along the sides. She ran water into the pan and said, "This is going to have to soak a while before it ever comes clean."

Toby looked over Jane's shoulder into the pan under the running water. "Yeah, like about two weeks." They both laughed.

Most of the evening's meal found its way to the garbage can to keep the bread company. The assembly line of dirty pots and pans seemed endless.

"I didn't know we were making such a mess," Jane said when Toby handed her another bowl.

"This is about the last of it," Toby said.

"Except for this." Jane pointed to the sticky broiler pan that was still soaking on the cabinet. "I'm afraid it's going to take a lot more than an S.O.S. pad to get this clean."

"Why don't we leave it soaking and clean it up right before we go to bed?" Toby suggested.

"Good idea," Jane agreed. She'd had her delicate hands in the harsh dishwater long enough. Toby put the last of the clean dishes away while Jane finished wiping down the cabinets.

Jane took the towel that had been around Andy's waist earlier in the day and dried her hands on it. Toby lifted the plastic garbage bag from the trash. "I'll take this out, and we'll be finished."

Toby pushed open the back door and was surprised to find the porch empty. She took the trash over to the big Dumpster near the barn. She heaved it in a wide arc and watched it sail into the darkness of the big metal container.

She looked around for Andy, but didn't

see her anywhere. She must have gone in through the front door, Toby thought. She pulled open the kitchen door. "Where's Andy?" Jane asked.

"She must have gone in the front," Toby said.

The two girls went into the living room. Mr. Houston was sitting in his recliner, reading the paper and smoking his pipe. He looked up at the girls and smiled. "All done?"

"Yeah," Toby said. "Did Andy come through here?"

Mr. Houston shook his head. "I don't think so. I didn't see her, anyway."

"We'll check upstairs," Toby said. She knew how her father was when he was reading the paper. A bomb could go off outside, and he probably wouldn't notice. It was the one time he let himself really relax all day.

Jane and Toby went upstairs. Toby pushed the door of their room open and called, "Hey, Andy, everything's all cleaned up. You want to . . ." But Andy wasn't there.

Jane came into the room behind Toby. "Where do you think she went?" Jane's worried voice asked from the doorway.

"She can't have gone far. She's probably out in the bunkhouse with Abe." But even as Toby said it, she doubted it. Just because she hadn't seen Andy didn't mean that Andy wasn't out there somewhere. She hadn't really looked that carefully.

They went back down the stairs. Her father looked up from his paper. "Did you find her?"

"Not yet, but we really haven't looked," Toby said. He nodded and slipped the pipe back between his teeth. He shook his paper out and went back to his evening's reading.

Jane followed Toby out the back door and over to see Abe. Abe was sitting on the porch of the bunkhouse, his chair leaning against a wall, smoking a cigar. He set the chair down on all four legs when he saw the girls approach.

"Evening, ladies. You out for a stroll, are you?"

"We're looking for Andy," Jane said. "Is she here?"

"Nope, haven't seen her." Jane sent a worried look toward Toby. "Where could she have gone?"

"I'm sure she's around here someplace," Toby said. She turned back toward Abe. "Thanks," she called as she ran off in the direction of the barn.

Max whinnied when he heard Toby's familiar voice calling out to Andy. Toby went over to his stall, hoping to find Andy huddled in the corner. The only thing in the stall was Max. "You seen Andy, boy?" she asked.

Jane said sharply, "Andy's missing and you stand there talking to a horse. We have to *do* something."

"We will," Toby said. "First we'll check all

around the house and then if we don't find her, we'll get in the jeep and start hunting for her."

"Well, whatever we're going to do, we'd better do it fast. It's getting dark."

Toby came out of the barn. The sun had completely set. They continued to search all the outbuildings around the ranch. Andy was nowhere to be found.

The moon was high in the sky and a coyote howled off in the distance. Jane instinctively grabbed Toby's arm. The two of them stood side by side looking out into the blackness. The night had settled over the prairie, and Andy was out there somewhere. Alone.

CHAPTER ELEVEN

"Are you sure you've looked everywhere?" Mr. Houston asked when Toby frantically relayed the facts about Andy being missing.

"I'm sure of it," Toby said. She paced around the living room, running her hands through her short red curls. If only she were the one out there, it would be okay. Toby knew the wilderness. She knew her way around; how to look out for herself. Andy, on the other hand, wouldn't have any idea of what to do. "I called and called her name and she didn't answer."

"Maybe she's still upset and she needs more time alone," he reasoned.

"She wouldn't do that," Toby insisted. "She wouldn't stay out there and pretend she couldn't hear me. She knows we'd worry. Something's happened. I know it has."

"Now, take it easy," her father said.

Jane popped up from the sofa where she had sat down only a minute before. She lifted the lace curtain away from the window and peered out into the night. It was so dark. How would Andy ever find her way back? What if she had gotten bit by a rattlesnake or a scorpion? Visions of Andy lying out there hurt and alone and helpless flashed through her mind. Jane shuddered and rubbed her hands vigorously up and down her crossed arms.

Bill Houston cast his newspaper aside and stood up. "I'm sure she's close by. She wouldn't go far. I'll get Abe, and we'll go out in the jeep and see if we can find her."

"What should I do?" Toby asked. "Maybe Max and I should take off in another direction."

"And I could go out and help, too," Jane volunteered, though the idea of going out in the night, even if she was searching for Andy, seemed terrifying to her.

"No, there's no need for anybody to panic. All I need is to find Andy and then come back here to find the two of you have wandered off and gotten lost somewhere. You just wait here in case she comes back."

Toby realized her father was talking about Jane, because he knew that Toby could never get lost out there. But she guessed he was right. Having Andy out there was bad enough, but having Jane out there would be worse.

At least when they had gone off together, Andy seemed to have been paying attention to where they were going, and she had asked several questions about the geography of the ranch. Andy wasn't terrified of every sound and every bug they saw. Toby stole a glance at Jane's finely chiseled features and tried to imagine her out there lost in the dark. No, if one of them had to be lost, it was definitely better if it was levelheaded Andy.

They stood on the porch and watched the jeep pull out of the yard. Jane listened to the night sounds around her. There were hundreds of insects and snakes and wild animals roaming this open prairie and poor Andy was out there wearing only shorts, a light cotton blouse, and tennis shoes. A shiver ran down Jane's spine. "I hope they find her soon."

"Don't worry," Toby said, putting her arm around Jane's shoulders and steering her back inside. "I'm sure they'll find her. She may not be lost. She might have just gone for a walk and went further than she planned." Toby glanced back over her shoulder into the night and prayed she was right.

But Andy knew she was lost. As she circled around the outcropping of rocks that she thought would bring her back to the ranch, she felt her heart sink. She had been sure when she got to the top of the rise, she would see the house off in the distance. Instead all she had found was more blackness.

She sat on the rock and let the tears roll down her face. Her head was pounding from the running and crying. She could feel the hungry mosquitos gnawing at her unprotected legs. She slapped at one of them, pulled her legs into her, and wrapped her arms protectively around them.

Why had she been so careless? When she had seen them all sitting around the table eating peanut butter sandwiches and laughing, she had felt betrayed and left out. She had fled into the night without paying much attention where she was running to. Now that she had calmed down, she tried desperately to remember which direction she had come from.

She stood up, balancing on the tallest rock, and looked in a wide circle all around her. Nothing. There were no lights, no buildings, no trees. Nothing. Just miles and miles of emptiness. Suddenly, she lost her footing and began to slide. Clutching frantically at the empty air, she slipped off the rock feeling the jagged edge scrape her leg on the way down.

She hit the hard ground with a bump and howled out her pain and frustration. In the distance, a coyote answered her cry. She froze. Her eyes darted in the direction from which the sound had come. How far off was it? A mile? A hundred yards? Would it attack her?

The jeep bounced along the empty prairie. Abe drove while Bill Houston scouted the horizon. Twice he had seen dead mesquites, their branches in almost human form, and thought he had found her.

They had started out toward the north pasture, Abe thinking that since he had taken the girls up there, Andy might be inclined to head that way.

Mr. Houston slid back onto the seat. "It's no use. It's so dark out here, I can't see more than fifty feet. It'll take all night to search this area at this rate. Let's head back."

"Are you sure?" Abe said. Bill Houston didn't answer him. Abe turned the jeep around and started back toward the ranch.

Andy jerked her head up. She had been dozing. She had heard something. A motor maybe? Was Toby out looking for her in the jeep? Favoring her sore leg, she limped to the edge of the rocks and again climbed high enough to see all around her. She couldn't see anything. No headlights reflecting into the night. With tears of disappointment, she slid back to the ground. She must have been dreaming.

"What do you mean you'll have to wait till morning?" Toby cried. "You can't leave her out there all night."

"The moon's hidden behind the clouds. There's almost no visibility."

"There has to be," Toby insisted. She remembered the time last winter when she had gotten upset with Meredith Pembroke, the new housemother, and had taken an angry ride on Maxine to free the feelings of claustrophobia she had been having.

Maxine had thrown her. She had landed in a snowdrift, her ankle sprained and swollen, unable to go for help. If Randy had waited until later, it would have been too late for her.

What if something had happened to Andy? What if Jane's worst fears had been realized, and she had been bitten by a rattler? She knew there were places on the ranch where they were plentiful. Toby also knew to stay clear of them. Andy wouldn't know that, though. They *had* to go back out tonight.

"Dad, what if she's hurt? We can't just go to bed and leave her out there."

Bill Houston sighed. Toby was right. Even if they didn't go back out, he wouldn't be getting any sleep. He might as well be looking for her. It was ten-thirty. He doubted she could find her way back, or she would have been there by now.

He walked over to the phone. "I'll call the Stocktons. The only way we'll stand a chance of finding her is if we can split up and take different directions."

Toby shot up the stairs with Jane right behind her. "Where are you going?" Jane asked.

"I'm getting into a pair of jeans and chaps. I've had enough of this sitting around. I'm going out on Max and help look for her."

"What can I do?"

"You can wait here in case she comes back and tell her to stay put."

Jane followed Toby into their room. She didn't like the idea of missing out on the search. But the thought of trying to find her way around the ranch at night was not appealing. If she went out they'd probably be looking for two girls instead of one.

Jane walked out onto the porch and watched Toby cut across the grass to the barn. Max whinnied at the sound of Toby's call. Jane could barely see the shadowy figure of Toby as she saddled Max in the corral.

Toby leaped easily into the saddle and rode out of the gate. She waved to Jane. "Wish me luck!"

"Good luck," Jane called after her. She wasn't sure who needed the luck more, Toby or Andy. It certainly was dark. The clouds were forming a canopy that was blocking most of the stars that had shone so brightly the night they had camped out.

Jane thought back on that night and shuddered. She had been so scared and yet they had been within sight of the ranch and she had had Toby and Andy right next to her. It was probably a good thing she wasn't the one lost out there. She really would have a heart attack, and they'd find her body in the morning.

The sound of horse's hooves turned her about sharply. Toby must have forgotten something. As the horse and rider moved into the light coming from the kitchen, Jane recognized the big golden horse that Beau Stockton rode.

"You okay?" he asked with concern in his voice. Jane was surprised. "When Bill called my dad and said one of the girls staying here had gotten lost, I was afraid it was you."

Touched by his interest in her well-being, she put her hand self-consciously to her hair and said, "I'm fine."

"Well, I'm gonna help them look. Do you know which direction everyone went?"

Jane got a brilliant idea. "Why don't I show you? I'll leave a note for Andy and we can look together. I feel so useless just sitting around here waiting for something to happen."

"Okay." He looked at her critically. "You got anything upstairs besides those shorts?"

"Yes, why?"

"Because you're gonna get chewed up some if we tangle with any brush tonight. You'd better get a move on."

Jane ran back into the house and upstairs as quickly as she could. She pulled her sweats from her suitcase and wished she'd bought a pair of jeans when they'd been in Rio Verde. She thought about wearing a pair of Toby's, but Toby was several pounds thinner and they'd probably be too tight.

She looked at the sweat pants in her hands. Oh, well, she thought, they are better than nothing. Besides, this wasn't a fashion show; she needed to get back down there and help Beau find Andy.

Beau was standing on the porch pacing nervously, when she came back down. He stared briefly at her sweats, started to say something, then thought better of it. He stepped around to the side of the horse and got on. He reached his hand down to help her up. "Okay, show me where they went."

Andy slapped at the persistent mosquitos that wouldn't leave her alone. She looked into the sky. It was so inky and spooky tonight. The stars were nearly blocked out by the cloud cover above her. Her leg throbbed where she had scraped it.

She had decided to wait until the sun came up and then start back toward the ranch. But she still had no idea which direction the ranch was. She knew that she could wander out here for days and not see another living human. Surely Toby wouldn't let her starve to death out here? They had to be looking for her. She strained to listen to the silence in the night, hoping to hear the sound of engines or horses. She heard nothing, save the crickets and flying bugs that were nearby.

Then she heard a different sound. Like a rustling. Or a rattling. The sound was too loud for any bug to make and there were no large trees near that would house the noisy cicadas. She didn't move a muscle. Even before her mind acknowledged it, she knew what that sound had to be. A rattlesnake. If she got bitten, she wouldn't have to worry about starving to death. The poisonous venom would do the job on her.

Where was the sound coming from? Why was it so dark tonight? Not wanting to make any sudden movement that might cause the snake to strike, Andy slowly rotated her head around and searched for the reptile that she knew had to be close by.

Beau and Jane rode into the yard shortly after Toby had come back. She was going to take a short break and get something to eat before going back out. She couldn't think of sitting around the safety and comfort of the house when she knew Andy was lost. She felt doubly guilty because it was her ranch and her lamp that had started all this.

Beau reigned his horse in and helped Jane down. He got off himself and landed on the ground next to her. He put a comforting arm around Jane's shoulders. "We'll find her," he said reassuringly.

They came up the steps into the kitchen. Toby stood up, the look of hope slipped off her face when she saw only the two of them. "No luck either, huh?"

Beau shook his head. "Well, have a bite to eat and we can head back out."

"How can you think about eating?" Jane said. "Andy may be hurt and at the very least, probably terrified, and you talk about eating?" Her voice cracked and she fled back out onto the porch.

Beau got up from the table and quickly followed her. "Hey, Boston, you surprise me. I thought you were too tough to cry."

He encircled her in his arms. She folded into him and felt the security he provided. She'd never felt so safe before. She looked up into his handsome face. He brushed a tear from her smooth cheek with his work-roughened finger. The touch of him sent a shiver down her and he held her close. "Are you cold?" he whispered.

The warmth of the day still hung in the air, and yet she couldn't stop shivering. Was it the fear for Andy or the nearness of Beau?

Toby had started out after Jane, then stopped at the door when she saw Beau could probably offer her more comfort and reassurance than she could. She envied Jane. She wished she had someone who would tell her that everything was going to turn out fine. But unlike Jane, she knew what Andy was up against out there.

Andy sat frozen in terror for what felt like hours. It was probably no more than fifteen or twenty minutes. She never could see the menacing snake. After the first initial warning of its rattles, she never heard it again, either. She was terrified to move in any direction. Now she'd have no choice but to wait for sunup.

Then she heard the same sound she'd thought she'd heard earlier in the night. It definitely sounded like an engine. She tried to scan the skies above her for airplanes but it was too cloudy. Anyway, the sound seemed to be coming from in front of her, not above her. Should she risk jumping up and yelling for help? The snake was still out here someplace, she was sure of it.

Abe stopped the jeep. "We've been out here before. I just don't think she could have come this far," he said, shaking his head. "Maybe we ought to turn and head east a while."

"You're probably right." Bill Houston ran his hands through his hair in the same nervous gesture Toby often used. "What time is it getting to be?"

Abe squinted at the luminous dial on his watch. "Nearly two. I know how you feel about finding her, but I really think we need to grab a couple hours sleep and start out at first sign of daylight. We've lost what little moon we had earlier and we're just running around like chickens without heads out here."

"I guess so. Turn her around."

Abe reached for the key. That's when they both heard the distinctive cry for help. Abe froze, his hand above the key in the ignition. He looked over at Bill Houston. They heard it again. Bill Houston stood up in the jeep and yelled, "Andy? Where are you?"

"Over here," she cried. "Hurry."

He sat back in the seat. "That outcropping of rocks to the left," he pointed. "Let's go."

Abe turned the key and the jeep turned over and hummed steadily. He gunned the engine and sped toward the outcropping. The head lights revealed Andy, sitting rigidly atop the rocks.

Bill Houston jumped from the jeep before it had even had a chance to come to a complete stop. "Careful!" Andy cried. "There's a rattler around here someplace," she hissed in a terrified whisper.

Mr. Houston stopped. "Shine that searchlight this way," he said softly to Abe, who was reaching into the glove compartment for the small twenty-two they kept there for protection. They heard the distinctive rattle. It was coming from the rock above Andy's head.

The light fell on the snake, which blended with the color of the rock. "Here," Abe said, tossing the pistol to Bill Houston.

"Don't move, honey," he whispered. "Sit very still." Mr. Houston took a cautious step toward Andy, then carefully aimed the pistol above her head. The pop of the gun wasn't as loud as Andy had expected, but still she screamed. She heard something drop into the ground not far from her and she sprang forward into Bill Houston's waiting arms.

He walked her to the jeep after she had calmed down and stopped crying. He soothed her with reassurances that she was fine now. She got into the jeep and had never been so glad to see anything in her life as the lights of the house in the distance.

CHAPTER TWELVE

Jane dozed fitfully against Beau's shoulder while Toby slept in the wicker rocker. Beau scanned the countryside for any signs of movement. In the distance, he caught sight of a flash. He wanted to stand up to a better vantage point, but looking down at the beautiful girl sleeping on his shoulder, he couldn't bring himself to disturb her.

He kept watch on the spot off to the north where he'd seen the flash. It was probably sheet lightning. He let himself close his eyes and surrender to his feelings of exhaustion mingled with the sweet feeling of the girl at his side.

Beau's eyes snapped open almost as quickly as he had shut them. Had he heard a car engine or had he been dreaming? He looked off to the right again and this time he was sure he saw something. Bouncing across the terrain were beams of light that had to be coming from the jeep. It could be Abe and Bill were just coming back for the night to catch some sleep and get a fresh start at sunrise. He decided to wait before he woke the girls.

The problem of waking Toby and Jane was taken out of his hands when a loud burst from the jeep's horn brought both of them up sharply. Toby got to her feet and went to the edge of the porch.

"What is it?" Jane asked sleepily.

"It's Dad's jeep. I hope they've found her."

Jane got up and stood beside Toby. Beau got to his feet and stood near her. He nearly reached out and put his arm around her to draw her close to him again, but there was something very forbidding about Jane when she was awake. Instead, he reached his long arms above his head and grasped the edge of the porch overhang, while they waited to see what news Abe and Bill Houston had.

Seeing the three of them on the porch, Abe blasted the horn again. Andy was waving frantically as tears of joy and relief rolled down her cheeks. Mr. Houston could have told her that no one could see them this far off with the darkness of the night, but he enjoyed seeing her excitement.

Abe hardly had a chance to pull the jeep to a stop before Andy leaped out. Toby and Jane flew down the steps of the porch with equal enthusiasm. The three girls embraced and cried and patted each other in a happy reunion.

Abe and Bill Houston stood off to one side and watched them. Beau came down to join them. Beau leaned over to Toby's father and said, "There's nothing I like better than a happy ending."

Andy pulled away from Jane and Toby. "Well, it's almost a happy ending. We have one more thing that will make it complete."

Jane and Toby exchanged puzzled glances as Andy ran into the house. Everyone followed her. She ran upstairs to the room while they stood in the kitchen below.

Andy pushed open the kitchen door. She had a shy grin on her pretty face and she was holding something behind her back. "The evening can't end until we give you the thing that started it." She produced the broken lamp which was now decorated with excess seams outlined in clear glue.

Bill Houston began to laugh. His laughter roared through the kitchen and filled the house. Toby stared at him in stunned silence for a moment. She hadn't know her father to laugh like that since before her mother had died. Pretty soon everyone was joining in the laughter, causing a mingling of voices drifting out of the big, old farmhouse and into the night.

Bill Houston took the lamp from Andy and sat down to examine it more closely. "You know," he finally said, "I think it's a great improvement."

When the laughter settled down, Andy cleared her throat and everyone looked at her expectantly. "I just want to say how sorry I am that I caused all this fuss tonight. I didn't mean to. I thought I knew where I was going. I tried to do what you said, Toby, you know, about following landmarks. When I saw the outcropping of rocks I thought I recognized where I was. It turned out to be the wrong rocks. I never meant for anyone to go to so much trouble."

Bill Houston was touched by her sincere apology. No wonder his daughter had been drawn to these girls. Just like Toby, they were pretty special. He got up and patted her on the shoulder. "That's okay, Andy. You're worth all the trouble you caused and then some."

"Well," Abe said as he stretched his hands high above his head and stifled a yawn, "I believe I might try to catch a few hours sleep before the sun gets up."

"Sounds like a winner to me," Bill Houston said.

"Guess I'll wait out here for a few minutes and see if my dad comes back," Beau said, indicating toward the back porch.

"That's right," Abe said, remembering they had gone east toward the Stockton place in search of Andy.

Jane looked at Beau and realized she wasn't the least bit tired anymore. "I'll come with you."

"You want us to come?" Toby asked.

"No, it's okay. Go on up to bed," Jane said.

"Well, if you're sure."

"I'm sure. I'll be up just as soon as Beau's father gets back."

Jane followed Beau out onto the porch. The night was still warm. Everyone else had gone to bed, turning off most of the lights until there was only the dim light filtering out from the kitchen onto the back porch.

Both of them felt awkward in the dark silence. Beau sat in the porch swing and Jane sat down beside him. "Tired?" she asked.

"Not really." His arm ached to stretch out and encircle her, but he couldn't bring himself to do it. He smiled at her and felt shy and foolish. He was no klutz around girls, but this one was so different.

Jane watched his profile in the faint light from the kitchen. He was so incredibly handsome. She remembered the feeling of sleeping against his shoulder and wished he would put his arms around her. Should she lay her head against him? No, that would be too forward. She'd let him make the first move.

Instead of drawing closer to her, he stood up and reached for the edge of the porch roof above his head and stood like he'd been standing when they brought Andy back. "You know, Boston, this has been some night. Bet you don't get this kind of excitement back home."

"Not usually. There aren't too many open spaces to wander off in around Boston."

"I guess not. I guess that's why I'd never live there."

Jane felt her pride beginning to stir and she got up to stand next to him. "How do you know you wouldn't like it? You've never even seen it."

"Nope. And I'm not likely to. I always say, 'Once you've seen heaven, there's no need to keep shopping around.' "

"Oh, you do, do you? Well, I'll let you in on a little secret. If my memory serves me right, heaven isn't the place that's hot twenty-four hours a day."

"Are you insinuating — "

"All I'm saying is if you're looking for heaven on earth, you'd better keep your eyes open. I don't think this is it."

"To each his own, Boston." He picked up his straw cowboy hat from the porch railing. "I'm going to ride on out toward home. I'll probably see my dad along the way. Might as well turn him back and let him get some sleep tonight."

He climbed onto his big golden stallion. "Take care, Boston, so we won't have to go looking for you next time." He turned his horse and galloped off into the darkness.

Jane felt her frustration building toward an angry scream. Why was he so impossible? He brought out the worst in her. It was a good thing he was so narrow-minded that he'd never leave Texas, because she'd probably never return, and the two of them would never have to see each other again.

She went into the house clinging to that thought. But rather than offer her the comfort she was seeking, it created an empty feeling inside her.

The girls slept until after ten the next morning. When Jane opened her eyes and looked across the space between the two beds, she saw Andy still sleeping soundly. Toby was getting dressed. Jane leaned up on one elbow and Toby put her finger to her lips in a signal to be quiet.

Jane threw the covers back and got out of bed. She followed Toby into the hall. "Where're you going?" she whispered.

"The rodeo's less than a week away, and I haven't spent near as much time getting Max ready as I should have."

"What do you have to do?"

"We should be riding the barrels every day. It's like anything else; you can't keep your time down if you don't work at it. Get dressed and come on down if you want to."

"Okay," Jane said. She went back into the room and pulled her clothes from the drawer as quietly as she could. She was stepping into her shorts when she heard Andy ask, "Where are you going? Off with Beau this morning?"

"Don't remind me," Jane said. "He is the most obstinate, ill-mannered boy I have ever met."

Andy rolled over and smiled up at the ceiling. "He sounds just your type."

"For your information, I am going out to watch Toby do whatever it is you do when you're getting ready to do what she does when she rides in a rodeo," Jane said in a huff.

"That sounds fun. Wait up and I'll go with you." Andy threw back her own covers, stepped down on her leg, and winced. She looked at the angry scrape of her calf. She had forgotten about it in all the excitement of the night before. She stepped down gingerly, thinking that it looked like she'd be wearing shorts for the next few days.

The sun was hot overhead when they went out to the corral to watch Toby working with Max. She had set up some big barrels in a clover formation and was furiously racing Max around them. When she rounded the last one, she dashed madly for the end of the pasture.

Jane watched her ride and wondered how she could go so quickly and not be scared to death. She thought about the apprehension she had felt in riding Beau's big stallion, and wished almost instantly that she had not.

Beau Stockton had been on her mind ever since last night. It was all wrong and she knew it. They had absolutely nothing in common. But then neither did she and Cary.

Just thinking about Cary brought a fresh sense of guilt down upon her. What would he think if he knew she had met someone who made her feel as excited and irritated as *he* had when they'd first met?

How would she feel if she knew he had met someone else while she was away? She wouldn't like it. Jane jumped from the fence. She needed to call Cary. She knew once she heard his voice, everything would be fine again. She could put that arrogant Beau Stockton right out of her mind.

"Where're you going?" Andy said.

"I have to make a phone call. Tell Toby I'll be back in a little while."

Jane drummed her fingers nervously on the counter while she listened to the clicks on the telephone line. The phone began to ring and she began to feel anxious. Maybe calling him was a dumb idea. She should hang up before he answered.

"Hello?" she heard on the other end of the phone. He had been sleeping. She'd woke him. She almost hung up. "Hello!"

"Hi, Cary, it's me."

"Me, who?" he asked, still not fully awake.

"Jane? Is that you? When did you get back from Texas?"

"I didn't. I'm still here."

"Wow. How do you like it? Last Saturday I was laying around with nothing to do and I ended up watching *Bonanza* on TV. I thought about you roughing it out there in Texas, and I had to laugh. Are you having fun, Jane?"

"Sure. How about you? Anything interesting going on back there?"

"Well, we practiced till really late last night. We've played a couple private parties. Not much action, really."

She tried to picture his long silky hair and his piercing blue eyes on the other end of the phone. But no matter how she tried to conjure him up, Beau kept appearing in her mind. She shook her head to rid herself of his image.

"Jane?" Cary said. "Are you still there?"

"What?"

"I said, when are you coming back? I'm anxious to see you again."

"Oh, a week from today. The rodeo's this weekend and then there's some kind of barn dance to wrap it all up."

"Barn dance?" he laughed. "You've got to be kidding me. Do they really have those? Well, take notes on the band and let me know if they're any good."

"I will."

"And Jane," he said.

"Yes?"

"Don't go falling in love with any goat ropers while you're out there."

Jane hung up the phone and stared at it for some time. She was afraid she already had.

CHAPTER THIRTEEN

The Saturday morning of the rodeo, the house was buzzing with excitement. Everyone had gotten up early and Abe had fixed a big breakfast. The girls had quickly gone through the dishes in order to get upstairs and finish getting dressed.

Toby got into her standard Wranglers and a western shirt that was cut to emphasize her figure. Andy was puzzling about what she should wear.

"It's going to be hot out there," Toby said. "If I were you, I'd wear shorts or something cool. You'll roast if you don't."

"But what about these?" Andy asked, holding up her new jeans.

"Save them for the dance tonight."

Toby went down to help load up Max, while Jane and Andy finished getting dressed. They came running down the stairs and Jane could hardly believe her eyes when she saw the clock in the kitchen. It wasn't even seven o'clock yet, and she felt so wide awake.

They went out to the corral where Abe and Mr. Houston were just finishing loading the horse trailer. Abe was driving the heavy pickup that pulled the trailer and the rest of them were going in the jeep.

The fairgrounds were just outside of Rio Verde. By the time they got there, cars and trucks and trailers were already overflowing from the small dirt parking lot.

Andy pulled herself higher on the seat and looked around. "Isn't this exciting?"

Jane was also looking around, but she was looking for one person in particular. She had no idea what kind of car his family drove. All she knew was his horse, and she doubted he would come riding up on that.

Toby hopped out of the jeep. "I have to go register," she said. "I'll meet you guys in the grandstands in a few minutes."

Andy and Jane followed Mr. Houston to the entrance to the grandstand and bought their tickets. "I'll get you girls settled, then go help Abe get Max ready," he said.

They found what Mr. Houston said were, "good seats" about halfway up and close to the middle. Jane looked around at the big dirt arena in front of her. Tractors were pulling an enormous rake across the ground to level it out. The United States, Texas, and Confederate flags fluttered noisily above their heads.

Shortly after Toby's dad left, Toby came up to the stands. "I can't stay long," she said. "I just wanted to let you know to wave at me in the procession."

"What's that?" Andy asked.

"All the riders open the rodeo by riding around the ring, then they stop and play the "Star-Spangled Banner," and then we're off."

"We'll watch for you," Andy promised when Toby got up to go back down to the rodeo floor.

She hadn't been gone long when the announcer said, "Ladies and gentlemen, welcome to the annual Rio Verde Rodeo. Today you will see some of the finest riders in Texas who will put you on the edge of your seats with live action that is a thrill a minute. Will you please stand for the opening ceremony?"

The music blared over the loudspeakers and the riders came pouring out of the gates three deep. They rode in a procession around the ring, splitting and going on either side before meeting up in the middle and coming back to the far end of the arena. A huge golden stallion came through the center of the riders carrying a flag, and the national anthem began to play.

Jane stared at the rider on the horse rather than the flag he was carrying. It was Beau and, in spite of herself, her heart raced at the sight of him.

The riders cleared the arena and the barrel racing began. Several girls came out and rode the cloverleaf of barrels just as Toby had been doing all week.

Abe and Mr. Houston had come back and were sitting beside them. Everyone leaned forward when they heard the announcer say that the next rider was, "Toby Houston, a fifteen-year-old, born and bred right here in Rio Verde." The crowd cheered as Toby came flying out of the starting gate.

She took the barrel to the left with lightning speed and rushed to the one on the right. Her foot might have caught the barrel, because it teetered dangerously and then righted itself. As long as the barrel didn't fall over there was no penalty. She urged Max on and he raced for the last barrel. She kept her turn tight and came racing back to the finish line. The official time was 14.3 seconds. The crowd cheered. It was the fastest time of the day so far.

There were still three other riders. After two of them had gone, it looked like it was in the bag for Toby. The last girl came out as quickly as Toby had. She circled the barrels with unbelievable speed. "She's gonna beat Toby's time," Abe said.

Then she got too close to the last barrel and it rolled drunkenly and fell over. The crowd let out a collective cry of disappointment. The penalty would cost her ten seconds. She still spurred her horse to the finish line with the same vigor she had shown all through the ride. Her time was 14.2, but the penalty had cost her the event.

Toby took her victory ride around the arena. Jane and Andy stood up and cheered the loudest of anyone when she rode by. She waved at them and shot a radiant smile in their direction.

The bronco riding was next. Andy watched it with excitement. Jane felt sure that that was the event Beau had said he was riding in. She kept listening for his name. When the event ended and he hadn't ridden, she wondered if he was all right.

Toby came back to the stands to be greeted by friends and neighbors patting her on the back and offering congratulations. Her father stood up and hugged her. "Great riding, honey."

Abe waited patiently for his turn and then gave her an equally big hug. "Sure glad to see you didn't lose your touch back at that fancy school."

"It'll never happen," Toby said. She climbed onto the seat behind them and sat with Jane and Andy. "What do you think?"

"I love it," Andy said. "It's so exciting."

"Yes, it is," Jane agreed. "I thought that Beau Stockton was riding in the bronco-busting event. I didn't see him."

"He rides bulls, not broncs. He's standing right over there against the fence," Toby pointed out.

Jane strained to see him over the heads of all the people milling around the gate area. She caught a glimpse of what she thought was his straw cowboy hat, but she couldn't really tell if it was him or not.

The calf roping began. Jane was still watching the straw hat she thought was Beau's and almost missed it when they said the next rider was Beau Stockton. Her attention snapped to the ring. Beau came out of the gate just after they released a small calf. He threw his rope around the calf and jumped from his horse. He made several quick circles with the rope and stood up to signal he was finished. He finished in just over eight seconds.

"That's good time," Toby said. "I doubt anyone can beat that."

Jane had her fingers crossed every time a rider came out of the chutes. Several of them came out early and "broke the barrier," as Toby called it, and got penalty time added to their score.

"That happens," Toby said. "One rider gets a really good time and the other riders are anxious to beat it, so they shoot out before they're supposed to and they get penalized."

The event ended and Beau still had the

best time. He took his victory ride just as Toby had done. Jane jumped to her feet with equal enthusiasm, unaware of the stares she was drawing from people around her.

Beau had seen her, too. He stopped briefly in front of her and tipped his hat. "You owe me a dance," he mouthed to her above the cheering crowd. He winked and rode on. Jane was suddenly so excited about the dance, she was wishing they had reached the last event.

Toby watched the exchange between Jane and Beau. Nothing could have surprised her more than the two of them hitting it off. If ever two people were ill-suited for one another it would have to be Beau and Jane.

Then she thought about herself and Neal. He was as proper Boston as Jane, and she was as typically Texan as Beau, and they seemed to get along well. Maybe there was something to that old saying that opposites attract.

The bull riding was the last event of the rodeo and one of the most exciting by far. "The rider has to stay on the bull for eight seconds," Toby said. "They draw for their bulls just before the rodeo begins."

"I bet they hope for a tame one," Andy said.

"Nope. They want a bull that'll give them a good ride and yet not be so wild they can't stay up."

The first three riders were thrown. Jane

caught her breath when the riders would fly into the air and come down several feet from the raging bull. The clowns would run out and distract the bull and allow the rider to leave the ring. One bull noticed his rider getting away and chased him all the way to the fence. When the rider hopped over the fence just ahead of the angry bull, the bull butted the fence in frustration.

"Is Beau really going to get on one of those?" Jane asked with an involuntary shudder.

"I think he's the next rider," Toby said. "Isn't that him in the chutes?"

Jane looked over and saw Beau sitting astride a huge black bull with wild eyes. There was a man at the gate and another standing on the fence near Beau. They were all talking so calmly. Someone said something to Beau, and he threw his head back and laughed. Jane could almost hear that laughter in her mind.

She found herself digging her nails into her palms as she waited for the signal to open the chute. The announcer began, "and now we have Beau Stockton coming back to try his luck on Black Thunder."

The chute opened and the bull was a blur of whirling, bucking motion as he tried to rid himself of the irritant on his back. Beau held tightly with one hand and swung the other in the air above his head.

"Why doesn't he use both hands?" Jane said nervously.

"He can't. The minute he puts that other hand on the ropes, he's disqualified."

"That's a stupid rule."

The bull went into a wild spin and Beau began to slip. Beau was bucked off and the bull continued to jump and spin for a second before he realized the rider was gone. Beau was getting to his feet and shaking his head, obviously dizzy from the whirling ride. The bull spotted Beau and raced toward him. His savage horn looked like it caught Beau in the side. Beau's legs crumpled and he went down.

Jane screamed and jumped to her feet. Tears filled her eyes as she watched Beau's inert body lying in the dirt. The experienced rodeo clowns danced and played with the bull to pull the animal's attention from Beau. The bull stood in the center of the ring, nostrils flaring, trying to decide between the body lying on the ground and the ones that were taunting him a few feet away.

He chose the live ones and charged at the clowns. The clowns expertly maneuvered him to the exit and out of the arena. The bull saw the open gate and ran for it.

The two cowboys who had been sitting near Beau before he went out were in the ring now kneeling over him. A hushed silence fell over the crowd. Jane's eyes were riveted to the arena, hoping to see some signs of life.

The two cowboys helped Beau to his feet and the crowd cheered. Beau took his straw hat from the ground and waved it bravely at the crowd. The boys helped a very shaky Beau from the arena. The next rider came out, but Jane's eyes followed Beau as far as she could see him. She watched the cowboys lead him out of the grandstands and into a waiting first aid trailer.

The announcer came on at the end of the bull riding and told everyone, "The Stockton boy is doing just fine. We had the doctor take a look at him, and it appears that kid's head is just as hard as his daddy's been saying. He may have a headache for a day or two, but there'll be no permanent damage. The horn missed him."

"I could have told them about his hard head," Toby said.

"Well, folks," the announcer continued. "This concludes the rodeo for another year. We hope to see all of you at the barbecue and barn dance later tonight, right here at the county fairgrounds."

"We better get Max loaded up and get home," Abe said. "We got about two hours to get cleaned up and get back here."

Toby accepted more congratulations as they left the grandstands. Andy was so excited at the prospect of a barn dance, and Toby was so preoccupied with all her well-wishers, that neither of them noticed Jane's loss of interest in the whole affair.

She was certain with Beau's mishap earlier in the day that he wouldn't be at the dance that night. She didn't want to go, either. She wanted to rush to his side and nurse him back to health. She wanted to hear his laughter like she'd imagined it when she watched him getting ready to ride.

But she was leaving on Monday. She was afraid she'd never hear that laugh again.

CHAPTER FOURTEEN

Andy looked adorable in her western outfit and ready to take on Texas at the barn dance. Jane had searched through her suitcase without much heart. What difference would it make how she looked? There would be no one there to see her.

She took the aqua sundress with the tiny spaghetti straps from her hanging bag in the closet. It wasn't very western, but it would have to do. She slipped into the dress and pulled the sides of her hair back from her face and caught it in an elastic band at the back, before she clipped the big aqua bow in place.

"You look beautiful in that color," Andy said.

"Thanks."

"Wait'll Beau sees you in that," Toby agreed.

"I doubt Beau will see it at all. You don't

really think he'd come to a dance tonight after what happened today do you?" she asked, feeling a shred of hope.

"Like that guy said, Beau Stockton is pretty hardheaded."

The girls went downstairs. Bill and Abe were waiting for them in the kitchen. It was the first time Andy and Jane had seen either of them in anything but work clothes. Even though Mr. Houston was wearing the same blue jeans and a western shirt, they were new and well pressed. Jane and Andy were both struck by how handsome he looked tonight.

He stood up when they came into the kitchen. "Well, I don't know when I've had the pleasure of three such pretty girls to escort for one evening."

"Don't get greedy," Abe said. He stepped forward and extended his arm. Toby took it while Jane and Andy took Bill Houston's arms.

The big covered picnic area was wall-to-wall tables with red-and-white checked paper covering them. The smell of the food cooking drifted into the open air and tempted their appetites. People were just getting in line.

Bill Houston reached into the back of the jeep and got the picnic basket. They chose an open spot on one of the tables and he handed out the plates. "Looks like we timed this just right."

The food was delicious. Everyone went back for seconds except Jane. She was too busy keeping an eye out for a familiar straw cowboy hat that never came.

While they packed up their picnic supplies, a platform was being set up at the front of the covered area. People began moving the tables off to the sides and out onto the grass. The band was warming up by the time they had finished rearranging things.

They began with a rousing chorus of "Dixie" which everyone knew the words to and went right into a thing called the Texas two-step. Andy studied the dancers going by and was busting to get out and try it herself. Suddenly, she couldn't contain herself any longer. She grabbed Abe by the hand and dragged him out onto the floor. Bill watched with an amused smile on his face. "That little girl can dance," he said.

"She sure can," Toby agreed.

"How about you and me?" he asked.

Toby looked at Jane who would be left alone. "Do you mind?"

"No, of course not. Go ahead."

She watched Toby and her father move with practiced skill to the music. The song ended and they went almost immediately into some other dance where the people formed lines about six deep and moved in a big circle around the floor, kicking and side-stepping. Jane watched in amazement as Andy picked the dance up almost immediately.

"I suppose I'll have to teach you that, Boston." Jane turned around to see Beau standing behind her, his foot propped on the bench. "Don't figure they do the Cotton-Eyed Joe back east."

"No, they don't." She could hardly hear her voice over the music and the pounding of her own heart.

"Well, what are we waiting for? Let's get your education started then, or did you forget you owe me a dance?"

"Are you sure it's all right?"

"Why wouldn't it be?" he asked with a puzzled expression on his handsome face.

"Because of today. Your accident. I — "

"Shoot. That was nothing. Come on, Boston, the song's gonna be over by the time we get out there."

He put his arm around her and began instructing her as to how to do the Cotton-Eyed Joe. She was so lost in his green eyes that she couldn't concentrate. But being with him left her floating, so she knew she could keep up with him.

The song ended to much clapping and cheering and Jane felt disappointed it was over. He had said "You owe me a dance," and she was sure that he had several other girls among these pretty Texas cowgirls that he had made the same promise to.

"Well, thank you," Jane said and started back to their table. The band had begun a slow country song and he grabbed her by the hand.

"Whoa, you aren't getting off that easy. I almost got myself killed out there today. I don't expect you to walk away after half of a dance."

She smiled and stepped back into his arms. They danced every dance up to the break. He taught her something called the Freeze and tried to teach her the Texas two-step. Both of them laughed a lot and finally gave up.

Toby sat on the sidelines and watched Jane and Beau. She had never seen either of them so happy. She wondered about Cary. What would he think of Jane's Texas conquest? Well, that wasn't her concern. Jane was finally having fun and that made Toby happy.

The band announced they were taking a fifteen-minute break. The crowd greeted the news with disappointed "Ahh's" as they began to clear the floor. Andy had danced almost every dance as well. But that was nothing unusual for her. She was probably the best dancer at Canby Hall.

Toby watched for Beau and Jane to come off the floor, but she didn't see them. Bill

Houston came back with glasses of punch for everyone. Andy took hers and drained it. "Whew, I needed that. It gets hot out there in these jeans. Jane was smart to wear a sundress." She looked around. "Speaking of Jane, where is she?"

"The last I saw," Toby said, "she was dancing with Beau. I lost track of them when everyone left the dance floor."

"If she's with Hal Stockton's boy, I'm sure she's fine," her father said. Toby had known Beau since kindergarten, when she'd beaten him up because he wouldn't give her the bat one day at recess. He had said baseball was for boys and she'd slugged him. Could that same obnoxious, loudmouth have a romantic side to him she'd never seen? It was hard to believe.

Jane and Beau sat on one of the deserted picnic tables at the edge of the grass. They had walked out there hand in hand, but he had dropped her hand and suddenly become shy when they sat down. "I like that dress," he said.

"It's not very western, I'm afraid."

"Well, neither are you," he said with a smile. "But that's okay."

The silence hung awkwardly between them. In the past, except for the night they had been searching for Andy, their relationship had been built on trading insults. Now, they sat together and didn't know what to say.

"How do you feel?" Jane asked.

"You mean right now?"

Jane nodded.

"A little warm, but that's to be expected," he said. "It's hot out tonight. You want some punch?"

Punch would have been nice, but she didn't want to take a chance he would leave and not come back. She shook her head.

"Me, neither," he said.

"I meant, how do you feel after the accident?"

"Oh, that. Well, it kind of rung my bell for a second or two, but I'm fine. You weren't worried, were you?" His familiar smile started breaking at the corners of his mouth.

"Not really, I . . . I just had never seen a rodeo before, and I didn't know anyone could get struck by one of those things and walk away from it."

"Happens all the time. Actually," he said leaning back on the table, "I arranged the whole thing."

"You did?"

"Sure. I bribed the bull and told him to make it look good. There was this fancy girl from Boston I wanted to impress."

"Oh, you," Jane said giving him a playful shove. He caught her hand and pulled her to him. Their lips met and it was as wonderful as Jane had hoped it would be.

They broke apart and she settled comfortably against his shoulder.

"You really are something, Boston," he said. "On the outside, you're pure ice and inside, you're all warm."

"Beau, could you do me just one favor before I leave?"

"Sure, what's that?"

"Could you call me Jane once?"

"Maybe," he smiled and kissed her again.

Jane and Andy slept in and went downstairs to the fixings of a big Texas-style picnic. "Grab your suits, girls. We're going down to the swimming hole for a day to remember," Bill Houston said.

Jane didn't go back up the stairs with quite the same enthusiasm that Andy did. She still had visions of the snake that had come too close for her comfort. She didn't care how harmless it was.

They all piled into the jeep and drove off across the ranch toward the swimming hole. Everyone but Jane took hold of the rope and swung out into the still water. They played volleyball, Abe and Toby against Andy and Bill. Jane refereed from the shore.

The game ended and Toby's father tried to persuade Jane to join them. "Maybe after lunch," she said.

"Sounds good. When do we eat?"

Jane turned and saw Beau leaning against

the big tree behind her. "Beau, I didn't expect to see you today."

"Disappointed?"

"No."

Everyone else was getting out of the water. Beau helped Abe set up the portable picnic table, while the girls helped Toby's dad get the food out. Dinner was a lively reenactment of yesterday's events.

Abe turned to Beau and said, "I was surprised to see you there last night."

"I had strong motivations for a quick recovery."

Toby watched him smile at Jane, who seemed lost in his attention. Toby still couldn't believe that this match had ever taken place. If she had been trying to match up her friends with the boys she knew around Rio Verde, Beau Stockton would have been the last one she would have thought of for Jane.

After dinner, Beau and Jane took a walk together. His hand found hers and she felt the warmth of it as it closed around her own. He stopped near a big, old tree and leaned against it. "Well, I guess this is it, huh?"

"What do you mean?"

"I suppose I won't see you again. Besides, someone as pretty as you has to have a boyfriend stashed away back in Boston." Cary's face flashed across her mind. Had she ever felt like this with Cary? Would Cary make her heart race like it was now when she saw him again?

Beau took the momentary silence to mean she did have someone else. "I thought so." He got up and turned away from her, pushing his hands into the pockets of his jeans.

"What about you? Don't tell me a big, good-looking rodeo rider like you doesn't have some cowgirl on the string."

He shook his head and looked back at her over his shoulder. "Nope." He looked at the sky through the tree above his head. "We'd better start back. I don't want them thinking I abducted you or anything."

When they got back to the swimming hole, everyone was packing up the jeep to head back to the ranch. "We were just wondering where you'd gotten off to," Bill said.

"Just went walking," Beau answered. He grabbed the other side of the portable table. "Here, let me give you a hand with that."

Toby moved over next to Jane. "Looks like memories aren't the only thing you'll be taking back to Boston."

"What do you mean?"

"I think you've got Beau Stockton's heart sewed up, too."

"You really think so?"

"I've known him for years and believe me, this has to be the first time I've ever seen him act like there might be hope for him."

"October Houston, I hope you're putting

in a good word for me," Beau said coming over to them. "I need all the help I can get on this one."

"Call me Toby and I'll think about it," she said getting into the jeep.

Jane started to follow Toby into the jeep, but Beau caught her hand. "I don't give up easily, Boston. You'd better tell that boy back east to hold on tight to you, 'cause if I ever make it out there, I plan to steal you away from him."

He leaned forward and brushed her lips lightly with his own. "Write me sometime."

"I will. I promise."

"And I might even call you one of these days." He walked her to the jeep. "Have a safe trip home, Jane." He winked at her and tipped his hat.

They sat on the porch and watched the sun set: Toby in the wicker rocker, Jane and Andy on the swing, and Bill Houston and Abe on the steps. "This has been some day," Abe said.

"It's been some two weeks," Bill replied. He looked over at the girls. "I guess I forgot how much fun it was to laugh. I'm gonna be real sorry to see you girls go."

"We'll be sorry to leave," Andy said. She looked at Jane, who nodded her agreement with tears sparkling in her eyes.

"Well, I hope you'll come back next summer. I know I'm not the only one who'd like to see you again." He smiled at Jane and she felt the blush go to her cheeks.

They all watched the sun drop behind the horizon and the soft light of dusk spread across the countryside. "Guess I'll be heading out to the bunkhouse," Abe said.

"Yeah, I haven't read the paper yet. Think I'll go on in myself. Good night, girls. See you bright and early in the morning."

They echoed his good night. No one spoke as they sat in the twilight. Each girl was lost in her own thoughts. Toby glanced at her friends and could see by the looks on their faces that she wouldn't be the only one taking memories of Texas back to Canby Hall this year.

Jane's 16th birthday turns out to be memorable for the wrong reasons! Read The Girls of Canby Hall #28, HAPPY BIRTHDAY, JANE.

The Girls
of Canby Hall®

by Emily Chase

School pressures! Boy trouble! Roommate rivalry! The girls of Canby Hall are learning about life and love now that they've left home to live in a private boarding school.

☐ 41212-4	#1	Roommates	$2.50
☐ 40079-7	#2	Our Roommate Is Missing	$2.25
☐ 40080-0	#3	You're No Friend of Mine	$2.25
☐ 41417-8	#4	Keeping Secrets	$2.50
☐ 40082-7	#5	Summer Blues	$2.25
☐ 40083-5	#6	Best Friends Forever	$2.25
☐ 40381-X	#12	Who's the New Girl?	$2.25
☐ 40871-2	#13	Here Come the Boys	$2.25
☐ 40461-X	#14	What's a Girl to Do?	$2.25
☐ 33759-9	#15	To Tell the Truth	$1.95
☐ 33706-8	#16	Three of a Kind	$1.95
☐ 40191-2	#17	Graduation Day	$2.25
☐ 40327-3	#18	Making Friends	$2.25
☐ 41277-9	#19	One Boy Too Many	$2.50
☐ 40392-3	#20	Friends Times Three	$2.25
☐ 40657-4	#21	Party Time!	$2.50
☐ 40711-2	#22	Troublemaker	$2.50
☐ 40833-X	#23	But She's So Cute	$2.50
☐ 41055-5	#24	Princess Who?	$2.50
☐ 41090-3	#25	The Ghost of Canby Hall	$2.50

Complete series available wherever you buy books.